LILA MACKAY finds life very unfair

ELECTRIC MONKEY

First published in Great Britain in 2026
by Electric Monkey, part of Farshore

An imprint of HarperCollins*Publishers*
1 London Bridge Street, London SE1 9GF

farshore.co.uk

HarperCollins*Publishers*
Macken House, 39/40 Mayor Street Upper,
Dublin 1, D01 C9W8

ISBN 978 0 00 851381 8

Printed and bound in the UK using 100% renewable electricity at
CPI Group (UK) Ltd
1

A CIP catalogue record of this title is available from the British Library

LILA MACKAY finds life very unfair

GILL SIMS

EMILY

CHAPTER ONE

I think Mum has been watching those cringe psychology TikToks about parenting and how to talk to teenagers. Poppy said she dreads getting in the car with her mum now, after her mum saw one that recommended using car journeys as the perfect opportunity to have difficult conversations with your teenager. Every time, even just if it's a lift to the station, Poppy's mum puts on a special 'caring' voice and asks Poppy if there's anything she wants to talk about, which makes Poppy just want to open the car door and jump out. Unfortunately, when Poppy said this to her mum, her mum got even more worried about Poppy and her teenage mental health and watched more TikToks on how to 'help' her. So now Poppy gets the bus to the station, so she doesn't have to talk about her feelings.

So far, Mum has spared me this, possibly because she doesn't really understand TikTok (she still insists on referring to it as 'the TikTok', even though I have told her repeatedly that calling it 'the TikTok' is *literally* the most boomer thing anyone could do – I suspect she is now doing it just to annoy me), but as we turned on to the motorway on our way to Dad's house, she cleared her throat in the way she does before she says anything serious, and then said, in a funny way that made me see what Poppy meant about her mum's special 'caring' voice, 'Emily, darling, you know you can talk to me about anything?'

I just grunted, and concentrated on staring at my phone, but Mum was not deterred and started explaining about how the car was a really good place to have these conversations because it was a neutral space and we didn't have to look at each other, we could just talk, and I couldn't bear it any longer.

'I knew it!' I burst out. 'You *have* been watching those parenting psychology TikToks, haven't you? Oh my God, it's so *unfair*! Why are you even *on* TikTok? You have, like, your old people's social media like Facebook and Instagram, why can't we just have TikTok? You never let me have *anything* for myself!'

'Old people's social media?' said Mum in outrage, though at least she was talking in her normal voice again. 'They are not old people's social media. Why would you even say that?'

'Because they *are*,' I pointed out. '*Literally* no one my

age uses them. Only you and your friends. And apparently that's not enough for you, because now you're taking TikTok too!'

'Why do you think I'm on TikTok?' Mum asked nervously.

'I *told* you. Because you're trying to do that "talk to them in the car" thing that the *old people* who are stealing TikTok from us are telling the other old saddos who are also invading our space to do. You know what this is? It's . . . it's *colonisation,*' I said in triumph. 'That's what it is. It's nothing more than *digital colonisation*. Dressed up as pop psychology, so you can embarrass your only daughter under the pretence of caring! You are the Christopher Columbus of TikTok! You are an *oppressor*.'

'I . . . what?' said Mum. 'I just asked if there was anything you wanted to talk about and now I'm some kind of colonial oppressor?'

'Yes. Because you're trying to steal our culture, and frankly, Mum, it's embarrassing,' I hissed. 'It's like that awful time you asked the security guard in the shopping centre where the skibidi toilet was.'

'I thought it was what the kids call the loo nowadays,' Mum protested. 'I was trying to speak his language!'

I despair of my mother. I have explained to her many times that no one says things like that except, like, really sad twelve-year-olds, and all Mum says is that the security guard had *looked* twelve anyway, so how was she to know?

None of this was helping my problem, though, as Mum was still determined to 'talk about things' with me, even though she claims she saw the car psychology video on Instagram, not TikTok. In fairness, she is probably telling the truth, because I have seen her trying to work TikTok, and sometimes I think it's no wonder she calls it 'the TikTok' because it is genuinely mortifying watching her. But as long as I kept arguing with her about it, I thought I might stand some chance of distracting her from the actual issue at hand that I knew she was dying to discuss.

I should have known better. My mother may not get TikTok, but she *is* tenacious.

I slumped in my seat and stared at my phone some more as Mum chuntered that I would make myself carsick, 'like that time you threw up blue icing all over the car after Erin's fourth birthday party because you'd raided the party bags while everyone was playing What's the Time, Mr Wolf? and eaten the icing off all the cake.'

Yes, Mum, I was *three*. I'm nearly fifteen now, do we keep having to bringing that up? Still, if I pretended I was feeling sick, then maybe Mum would let things drop and we could spend the rest of the drive to Dad's house in a vaguely companionable silence. Before I could give a sufficiently pathetic, nauseous groan, though, Mum had started again.

'Look, Emily, I know you're hurting, and you say you don't want to talk about it, but I think it would help. You think you're escaping things by running away to your dad's, but you can't ignore what's happened – you have to work through it. And that's what I'm here for.'

'Mum!'

'Emily, I know this is hard, your first break-up, your first heartbreak –'

'Great, Mum, thanks, just keep reminding me – Emily got dumped!' I snarled. 'Thanks a lot! And FYI, I am *not* heartbroken, I am TOTALLY OVER HIM! Literally could not care less. He saved me the trouble of dumping him, actually.'

'Emily –'

I stuck my headphones in and turned the music up, before Mum could attempt any more emotional bonding. I did not need this. Not right now. What I needed was to try and convince the world that I am completely over Oli Letby, that he means nothing to me, that he *meant* nothing to me. That all we had was a casual situationship, and that I am completely *fine* with it coming to an end.

Of course, I am not. I am shaken, hurt, shocked and humiliated. I thought he cared about me. I thought this was *it*. I thought we were going to be together forever – or at least until the end of school. But we didn't even make it to the end of the summer disco.

With hindsight, I should've seen it coming. Oli had been a bit weird for a few days. He's in the year above me, so during the week I only saw him at break and lunch, because Mum won't let me go out on a school night (so unfair). When we first started going out, he would be waiting for me, or looking for me when I came out of class. But towards the end of term, I started having to look for *him*. Then, he'd be hanging out with his friends instead of me, and I'd almost feel like I was intruding, or annoying him by being there. I told myself I was imagining it, I was his *girlfriend*, of course he'd want me to be there, why *wouldn't* he?

And then, it was the end of term summer disco. I'd hoped he'd offer to pick me up, or at least meet me first, so we could go together. I'd had vague ideas about him bringing me flowers, like in the films before they go to Prom, even though this wasn't a prom, just a summer disco, because we don't get a prom until Year 12. Mum develops an eye twitch every time someone mentions Prom, and goes off on a rant about how it's a DANCE, not a prom, that a prom is a ghastly Americanisation and entirely unnecessary and we are not the fifty-first state yet, and then she complains for a while about Starbucks too, though I can't really see what that has to do with Prom. Anyway, all such hopes were dashed when Oli just mumbled something after school about how he'd maybe see me at the disco, and then got on his bus, like nothing special was happening at all!

I had turned down Poppy's invitation to come and get ready at her house, so sure was I that I'd be going to the disco with Oli, but Poppy was standing there beside me when Oli said he'd 'see me there' and she's such a good friend she didn't even make a big deal about it and say, 'Well, sucks to be you, loser,' or any of the other things she could've said, given I had picked Oli over her (and more than once this term, I have to admit, to my shame). Instead, she just said, 'Hey, I don't suppose you've changed your mind about coming over to get ready, have you?' so I was able to totally casually just pretend that actually, yeah, that would be great.

We got to the disco and Oli was even weirder. Every time I sat down next to him, he made some excuse and disappeared. He was going to get a drink, or he needed the loo, or he just had to talk to someone quickly.

Eventually, towards the end of the night, Mr Bryant, the geography teacher slash DJ for the evening, put on some slower music and people started dancing together.

I looked hopefully at Oli. He sort of winced and then he said, 'Emily, we need to talk.'

I felt like I was in a lift plummeting at high speed and I'd left my tummy several floors above. *Everyone* knows no good can come from someone saying that to you. No one says, 'We need to talk,' before declaring their undying love, or announcing they're giving you a million pounds or getting you a puppy. 'We need to talk' could only mean one thing, so at least I had about forty-five seconds to compose myself as Oli shuffled his feet and said, 'Maybe we could go outside?'

I tried to tell myself that I was wrong. If he wanted to go outside, perhaps it was just so he could kiss me in the summer moonlight, and he wanted to talk about – oh, I don't know, my advice about his A-level choices or something. But I still had the horrible whooshing left-behind tummy feeling and I knew deep down what was coming.

I wish I'd trusted my instincts, and when we went outside, instead of looking at him, all big pathetic pleading eyes, hoping desperately that he wasn't going to say what I thought he was, I had just casually turned to him on the steps of the school hall and said, 'Actually, Oli, I don't think this is working, I don't want to see you any more,' and then at least *I* would have dumped *him*. I would still feel horrible, obviously, but I would have retained some dignity and control over the situation and felt like at least I'd been a good feminist and not a feeble little tool of the patriarchy.

Instead, I smiled at him like nothing was wrong and this was a totally normal way for him to behave at the summer disco, as he shuffled some more and then blurted, 'I don't think we should see each other any more!'

I couldn't stop myself. Before I even really knew what I was saying, I had whined, 'But *why*?', losing the last opportunity to play it cool and pretend I didn't care.

'Well, because, you know, this was only ever going to be, like, a situationship?' Oli muttered. 'Wasn't it? It couldn't be anything else.'

'Why not?' I was fighting back tears.

'Emily, please don't make this harder than it has to be,' Oli pleaded, like I was the one doing something hurtful to him.

'I'm not,' I sniffed. 'I just . . . I don't understand.'

'Well, it's obvious, isn't it?' he said. 'I'm going to be sixteen in a few weeks. And once I'm sixteen, I'll want someone who . . . well, you're not even *fifteen* yet, are you? And, like, that's not even legal, is it? I want to be a doctor, I can't get in trouble for something like that, can I?' Oli put on a very brave and martyred expression.

I gulped. 'Are you saying . . . that you want . . . ?'

'Someone with a bit more . . . maturity,' he said. 'Yes. Someone who can . . . you know.'

'Sex,' I said flatly. 'You're dumping me because you want someone old enough to have sex with, aren't you?'

'It sounds *bad* when you put it like that,' complained Oli, 'but, well, yes, sort of. I'm nearly old enough, I deserve to have that, don't I?' He did the brave, martyred face again.

'No one *deserves* it. It's not some *human right*!' I chuntered. 'Not unless you're some awful toxic masculinity sort of person!'

Oli was indignant as he went on to explain that, really, he was one of the good guys, that he was doing this *for me*, that he was *only thinking about me*, because he cared about me.

'If you *cared* about me,' I said bitterly, all attempts to keep the tears back failing as I wiped my nose with the back of my hand in a very unattractive way, 'you'd wait till I was old enough, and I was ready, instead of just *thinking with your trousers*.'

'That's very unfair,' Oli huffed. 'I told you, I'm thinking about *you*. But if anything, you're proving my point by being so immature now! You'll understand when you're older.'

'Whatever.' I wiped my nose again and turned my back on him to walk away with as much dignity as possible when you've just been dumped because, now your alleged boyfriend is going to be the grand old age of sixteen, he deserves so much more from a girl.

Once I was out of sight and earshot of the school hall, I gave into proper howls of woe. I texted Poppy, asking her to get my things and come and meet me, while I wept and wept, becoming more and more soddenly snotty, until Poppy appeared with my bag, which luckily had a packet of tissues in it. She mopped me up and hugged me while I gulped and sniffled some more, and then when I tried to explain, she said, 'It's OK, Emily. I think I can guess. He dumped you, didn't he?'

I nodded sadly.

'Alexa Neville said he was going to.' Poppy invoked the name of our arch-nemesis, the blonde, popular, utter *bitch* that was Alexa Neville.

I was aghast. Poppy had *known* this was going to happen? I wasn't sure what was worse: that Poppy had known before me, or that Alexa had.

Poppy quickly assured me that no, she'd had no idea, until Alexa saw Oli and I going outside together and had wasted no time in informing everyone that Oli Letby was off to dump Emily Osbourne because she was too immature for him and didn't put out. And, according to Alexa, after he'd chucked me he was going to get together with Grace Walker in his year, who apparently had all the 'maturity' I was lacking.

I burst into tears again, and then had to pull myself together when Mum rang to say she was in the car park to pick us up, and where were we?

I think it must have been quite obvious to Mum what had happened when she saw my tear-stained face, because she didn't ask where Oli was, even though we were supposed to be giving him a lift home too. Let him walk, I thought crossly, and then nearly started crying again in the car as I thought that soon enough he would be Walkering. It wasn't even a good pun. I was too upset for puns. Mum also tactfully didn't say anything to me while Poppy was in the car, but once we'd dropped Poppy at her house and we were home, she did try the 'Would you like to talk to me?' approach but I just told her I was tired and thought maybe I was coming down with something and that I wanted to go to bed. Luckily she didn't argue.

I was so relieved that at least the disco had marked the end of term and the school year, so I didn't have to go to school and face everyone the next day, but there was still a whole summer to get through, with every chance of bumping into Oli and Grace and the vile and hateful Alexa, who'd definitely get in some little dig at me whenever she could.

If I could just vanish for the summer and reappear in the autumn, I thought, maybe everyone would have forgotten that I was the girl who got dumped at the summer disco. Maybe, even, I thought hopefully, if he had a bit of time without me, Oli would realise he'd made a mistake, that Grace was shallow and mean and I was worth a million of her (I had no idea what Grace was actually like, I had never spoken to her, she might have been a saint who spent her spare time rescuing orphaned kittens for all I knew, but I preferred my version of her). Then, when we went back to school, Oli would fall dramatically to his knees in the corridor, *in front of everyone* (especially Grace and Alexa), and beg me pitifully to take him back.

Ha. There was a scenario. Would I take him back? Or would I say something cutting and scornful and make as big a fool of him as he had of me? That was what I *should* do, I thought. That was what a good feminist would do. But maybe he would have changed and I would smile kindly on him and he would sweep me into his arms and kiss me there and then and we would live happily ever after. (Except if Mr Stevenson the head caught us snogging in the corridors, it would be detention for us both, not a happy ever after.)

But first I had to enact stage one of my plan: Operation Stay With Dad for the Summer.

Mum and Dad both capitulated to my request with less objection than I'd been expecting. I was quite insulted, actually, at how easily Mum gave in and said, 'Yes, of course, Emily, if that's what you want, I'll ring him now and see what he says.' I do think she might have looked a *bit* woebegone and sorrowful that her only daughter would be spending the summer a hundred miles away. But no, she came off the phone to Dad positively *beaming* and just said, 'Well, this has worked out perfectly. I can spend time working on the edits to my novel without worrying about you being bored, and Dad's thrilled – he says you can come to the university and help him; it will be good work experience and something to put on your UCAS form!'

What? No. That wasn't part of the plan! I didn't want to help Dad in his boring office with his boring job all summer. First, I wanted to pine in an emotionally dramatic manner, and then, maybe, when I was looking suitably grief-stricken and interesting, some handsome boy would see me and fall hopelessly in love with me, and pursue me in a romantic but non-creepy or stalkery way, even though my heart was broken and I could never love another, but still, it would be nice to have some validation that I am lovable and do not repulse men. How was that supposed to happen if I was stuck at Dad's work, no doubt given some incredibly tedious task that Dad would pretend was vital and important, but really, no one else wanted to do? (Dad is a lecturer in archaeology and that is not as interesting as it sounds, because as far as I can see, his job involves not Indiana Jones-style adventures, but an awful lot of boring paperwork.)

I did object to this plan, but Mum just said briskly that everything was arranged now, she was sure I'd have fun once I was there, that the change would be good for me, and she'd arranged to drive me over on Sunday.

So that is how I ended up en route to a summer of being a general dogsbody, with probably no time to think about how sad and lonely I am. I told Mum I wanted time to 'think about things' at Dad's and I didn't feel like that was going to happen if I was always working, and Mum just said, 'There will plenty of time to think about anything at all, but if you have nothing to do all summer, you'll end up *over* thinking, and dwelling on things, and that is not healthy.'

Which is proof, if any was needed, that Mum has no idea what I am going through.

When we got to Dad's house, Mum and Dad were both very jolly and jovial, but when I was coming back from the loo, I heard her say very quietly to Dad, 'I just don't know how to get through to her, Andrew. Perhaps you'll have more luck,' and Dad spluttering, 'How I am supposed to know what to say to her about stuff like this?'

Great, so now Mum has told Dad what happened, and he will probably also watch TikTok videos about talking to your teenager, and then I'll get the special 'caring' voice from him too! It's so unfair; all I wanted to do was come here to lick my wounds in peace.

We waved goodbye to Mum, and Dad immediately turned to me and did the Voice, saying, 'Emily, you know you can talk to me about –'

'I need to unpack!' I said quickly, and stomped upstairs to my room.

At the top of my bag I found a small package and a note from Mum.

Darling Emily,

I know right now you are heartbroken and think everything is very unfair and life will never be the same again. And yes, in some ways that's true: you will be older and wiser and stronger after this. And I know that sounds unlikely, because at the moment you feel like this is something you will never get over, but I promise, you will. As the old saying goes, 'This too shall pass.'

I remember it helped you to read my old diary a few months ago, when you felt no one understood what you were going through, and then you realised that maybe you were not the only person to struggle with first love. Well, you are not the first person to have their heart broken either, and I thought that perhaps you would like to read my diary from the first time it happened to me? It's here if you want it. I'm here whenever you want to talk too, or if you want to come home – all you have to do is pick up your phone (like you ever put it down ☺).

All love, always,

Mum xxxx

I opened the package. Sure enough, it contained not a stack of H&M gift cards to cheer me up with retail therapy, but a small, battered book, the cover smothered in stickers and doodles, and the pages inside crammed with loopy teenage writing, so different from Mum's hurried adult scrawl. Mum's diary. Well, *Lila's diary*, as the cover proclaimed, along with ***PRIVATE AND CONFIDENTIAL.***

Lila again.

I still found it almost impossible to equate my mother with the sparky teenage girl in the pages of the diary Uncle Tom had given me to read last Easter. *That* Lila had become a friend, in some weird way. And now she was back, and she'd had her heart broken too. Did I want to know what happened? What if she wasn't the fun, silly Lila any more, but already someone more like Mum?

I had lost Oli. Was I willing to risk losing Lila too?

I was still trying to decide what to do, when Dad shouted up the stairs that dinner was ready. Dad's cooking is not a patch on Mum's, but I thought I'd better appreciate it while I could because his food is a million times better than his girlfriend Stella's.

Stella is a vegan, but I don't think that's anything to do with why it's so awful. I've had plenty of yummy vegan food, just none of it cooked by Stella. Unfortunately, whenever Stella is at Dad's, which is quite a lot, as she has been hinting very unsubtly about moving in ever since they got together, she insists on cooking, because she is under the impression her food is a) healthy and b) edible. It is neither.

Since Stella was currently on a holistic yoga retreat in the Lake District, Dad had made us cheesy pasta. He was very pleased with himself, saying, 'I've made your favourite, Emily,' and I was so relieved about NOT having to eat Stella's lentil bake that I didn't have the heart to tell him that cheesy pasta hadn't actually been my favourite since I was about five.

Alas, Dad did the whole, 'Emily, darling, do you want to talk?' thing again, which sort of spoiled the pasta.

I thought it was a good opportunity to tackle a subject I *was* keen to discuss, though, and so I twirled my spaghetti (Dad did not seem to realise that cheesy pasta is supposed to be made with penne, in his opinion 'pasta is pasta') round my fork, did my best innocent face and said, 'Well, now you mention it, there is something I'd like to talk about . . .'

Dad choked slightly on a bit of rocket from the token salad he had dumped out of a bag into a bowl so he could tell Mum and Stella that we had been eating vegetables, and once he'd finished spluttering and coughing, he carefully rearranged his face into that of a concerned father rather than one startled that his teenage daughter was actually going to discuss her *feelings* with him.

'Of course, darling, you can talk to me about anything,' he gulped miserably, taking a slug of wine to give him some Dutch courage for whatever horror I was about to unleash on him.

'Can I have a glass of wine?' I asked hopefully.

Dad perked up in the hope that this was my Big Topic for discussion, and said, 'No, you're only fourteen.'

'Nearly fifteen,' I argued. 'In France –'

'We aren't in France, Emily, we're in Surrey,' Dad pointed out. 'Was that what you wanted to talk about?'

'No,' I said. 'I wanted to know if you're going to marry Stella?'

Poor Dad choked again. This time, I was a bit worried he might be a goner. Finally, he gasped, 'Why do you ask that?'

'I was just wondering.' I had a forkful of cheesy pasta. It wasn't bad, actually. 'She's here a lot. That means it's serious, doesn't it? I've met her. I don't usually meet your girlfriends. So are you going to get married?'

'God, NO!' said Dad, before he could stop himself. 'I mean, um, it's complicated.'

'How?' I demanded. 'Are you just using her for sex? That's so misogynistic, Dad, you should be ashamed of yourself!' MEN, I thought in disgust. They were all the same.

Dad spluttered some more as he said, 'It's complicated,' again, before finishing up with how I was too young to understand and I'd get what he was saying when I was older.

I rolled my eyes at this patronising remark and shouted, 'Why does everyone say that to me? I'm NEARLY FIFTEEN! I understand plenty of things RIGHT NOW! It is SO UNFAIR that everyone treats me like a BABY!' And I flung my plate in the dishwasher and stormed off to my room.

I threw myself down on my bed and reached for my phone to pour out my woes to Poppy, but realised to my fury that I'd left it in the kitchen, and would have to go back down to get it. At the top of the stairs, I heard Dad on the phone to someone, talking very quietly in that stupid 'caring' voice, and I realised the person at the other end was Mum when I heard him say, 'Yes, I see what you mean, Lila, she *is* at a very difficult stage. Well, I'll do what I can, of course, but if you can't get through to her, I don't see what difference I will make. Perhaps I should get Stella to talk to her? What? Well, Stella's a woman, isn't she, she might be better at this sort of thing than me? OK, Lila, OK, there's no need to be like that about it. I just thought another female perspective . . . ! No, fine, I won't get Stella to talk to her, if you think it's a terrible idea. Actually, talking of Stella, she's calling me now, I'd better go. Yes, I'll let you know how I get on. Bye, bye. Stella! Hello, darling! Yes, she's here. Mmmm, she's being a bit tricky, to be honest with you. I think –'

I couldn't bear to hear any more about what Dad thought, or even worse, what Stella thought. My phone would have to wait. I couldn't go down there while they were all discussing me and how *difficult* I was. They would be *difficult* too, if they'd had their hearts broken like me.

I flopped down on the bed and wondered what to do until Dad finished talking to Stella and I could go and get my phone. My eye fell on Mum's package – *Lila's diary*.

I bet Lila would understand heartbreak and sorrow. And I did feel a pang of gratitude to Mum for intervening in Dad's appalling idea to get Stella to talk to me.

I sighed and picked up the diary.

It wasn't like I had anything else to do.

LILA

CHAPTER TWO

SUNDAY 7TH SEPTEMBER 1997

Tomorrow we start Upper Sixth. *Upper Sixth*. I can't quite believe that Jas and I have finally reached the heady heights of the Upper Sixth. I still remember quite clearly the day Mum and Mrs Chatterjee dropped us off together on the first day of primary school. And now, in less than a year's time, we will be done with school, and college, and everything familiar and safe and comfortable, and we will be cast out into a cold, cruel, unfeeling world to fend for ourselves!

Mum said I was being overdramatic when I announced this at lunchtime, and to my annoyance, Jas agreed with her, which I felt was most disloyal. Mum was her very briskest, doctory self as she said I was making it sound like I was being abandoned at the workhouse door and left to work my freezing little fingers to the bone for a dry crust of bread, instead of having to deal with filling in my UCAS form and making some decisions about universities and courses.

'But then you will cast me out,' I pronounced gloomily.

'If you call supporting you through university "casting you out", Lila, then yes, you are being cast out,' Mum said. Then she went on about how most people would call it 'encouraging you to spread your wings and see a bit more of the world', rather than staying in what last week I'd called 'the provincial backwater hellhole' I claimed she'd 'forced me to waste my life in'. Then she told me to stop being silly and eat my cheese toastie before it went all cold and soggy.

I sighed and took a sorrowful bite. Mum's warning had come too late; it was already cold and soggy. I pointed out what greater sign of my emotional distress than that I'd let a toastie go cold, but Mum and Jas were having none of it.

'It will serve you right if I pine away,' I told them. 'Perhaps I will stop eating and waste away and then you'll be sorry.'

Mum chuntered on about how letting one toastie go cold because I was too busy talking (a toastie she noted I was still managing to eat, despite it being cold), did not mean I was 'wasting away' and 'pining'.

'Is this about Nicholas?' she demanded. 'I do wish you'd make up your mind. You spent years and years refusing to so much as acknowledge his existence, and now he's not here, you claim to be "pining away"! You, my girl, are the living embodiment of the old woman who lived in a vinegar bottle!'

I gasped, stung by such cruel words from *my own mother*, as Jas asked who the old woman who lived in a vinegar bottle was, and Mum explained it was a children's story she used to read to me, about an old woman, funnily enough, who lived in a vinegar bottle (why she lived in a vinegar bottle was never made clear) and who, on receipt of being granted some wishes, wished for more and more, because she was never satisfied with what she had, until the good fairy grew so exasperated with her increasingly outlandish demands (I think she finished by wanting to be Empress of the Whole World) that the fairy plopped the ungrateful old woman back in the vinegar bottle and was done with her. How terribly unfair to compare me to her! I don't want to be Empress of the Whole World (though if someone *offered*, I probably wouldn't say no, I expect I'd be very good at running the world, better than the men that are trying to, anyway), I just want Nicky to come back.

I could kick myself for taking so long to realise that Nicky was The One. All the years I spent calling him Weird Nicky, and thinking of him as no more than the speccy, ginger, awkward nerd next door, and then, all of a sudden, it turns out he is the love of my life. I don't know what I was thinking all that time, because Nicky is not any of those things. He is lovely and kind and funny, and his eyes are sea green and his hair is not ginger at all, but a gorgeous dark red. And then, less than a year after I realised all this, and we had the *most magical kiss* at the college Christmas ball, under a tree in the starlight – my first kiss in fact, and boy, was it worth waiting for, because we were so *right* together and I just knew we were going to live happily ever after – he is gone!

Jas says this makes it sound like he's dead, not in Ohio, and Jas also says that she thinks all this nonsense about living happily ever after with the first boy who kissed me is ridiculous and very unfeminist of me, but what does she know? She's never been kissed by anyone as wonderful as Nicky. So why, why, WHY did his *stupid* father have to take a *stupid* job in *stupid* Ohio, and why did there have to be a school there for Nicky, so they could all go, and why did Nicky have to be so bloody clever that no one was worried about the effect on his results of moving continents and schools halfway through his A levels? And most of all, WHY did this have to happen to me? (And Nicky, of course.)

Everyone said, 'Oh, it'll be fine, you can write! You can email! A long-distance relationship might be fun!' How?

How exactly is a long-distance relationship fun? Getting letters instead of snogging is practically Victorian! It's what Jane Austen probably did ('I think she was Georgian?' Jas said, which was to entirely miss the point of my angst!). Letters will just not cut it. Neither will emails.

Apart from anything else, before Nicky was snatched so cruelly from me by uncaring Fate ('Seriously, Lila,' Kate said, 'do you have to be *quite* so dramatic about everything?'), we had been talking about taking things a little further between us. Going, in fact, what the Americans call 'all the way'. And now? Now he's in OHIO, surrounded, no doubt, by perky blonde cheerleaders with dazzlingly white teeth and swishy hair, waving their pompoms in his face and doing backflips and making it clear they will go anywhere he wants.

What is even the *point* of Ohio? It sounds like a made-up place. What has even happened there? Nicky, being Nicky, solemnly informed me, when I wailed this at him, that Ohio was the birthplace of seven US presidents, and the 'home of aviation' as the Wright brothers were also born there. Big wow. Who cares? He could be here with me, instead of in the birthplace of dead presidents and dead aviators.

And now we go back to college tomorrow, and I have to do it by myself, with no darling Nicky always there to have my back, looking out for me, making me laugh. All my friends, but especially Kate and Jas and Tom, pointed out that I am hardly alone and palely loitering, I still have them, and I know that's true, but it's still not the same.

Last year, when Jas and I started college after five years of incarceration ('Incarceration, Lila? Really? That's how you're referring to your time at a very pleasant day school?' Mum said) in an all-girls school, so excited to meet boys and grow up and get on with our lives, it turned out that the boy who was meant for me was someone I had known all along, since Nicky had lived next door to us for as long as I could remember. But that's hardly the point, the point is that last year we had started with such hope and anticipation, and this year I feel like there's nothing to look forward to, just an endless, hopeless vista of ennui stretching ahead of me, broken only by the jagged rocks of UCAS forms and exams, upon which all my youthful dreams would no doubt find themselves shipwrecked ('At what point when she's carrying on like this does it become acceptable to kick her very hard?' Kate had asked Tom yesterday).

It's all right for Kate and Tom. They haven't lost the love of their lives.

Kate pointed out yet again that it is 1997, not 1697, and there are many, *many* ways to communicate with Ohio. And Tom gently reminded me that at least I can be openly broken-hearted about Nicky's departure, whereas when Giles Atkinson, the rugby captain, had ended his brief and clandestine relationship with Tom, we were the only ones who had even known they'd been a thing, and Tom had had to keep his feelings to himself in public, as 1997 or not, neither of them were ready to come out to their parents or the rest of the college. This was terribly sad for Tom, of course, and very unfair that he was still so fearful of people's judgements and attitudes (I grudgingly conceded that it was sad for Giles as well, but it was less sad for him because he was rather pompous and annoying, and not a very nice person, and I had not considered him good enough for Tom anyway).

I know Tom has a point. And I know I'm starting to annoy my friends. Even Tom, usually so kind-hearted, briskly suggested that maybe I should focus on all the things I *do* have, instead of bleating (*bleating!*) about the one thing I don't have.

'Like what?' I demanded. 'And if you say "my health", I will kick you!'

'Like the months you've had with Nicky, wrapped up in each other,' said Tom patiently. 'Hell, wrapped *around* each other half the time. You're lucky to have found such a special relationship – look at what happened to poor Jas and Mark.'

I had to concur; I *had* been lucky. Last year Jas had fallen head over heels for Mark, who initially had seemed to be just as into her, before suddenly and callously dumping her amid spurious claims that he needed 'space'. We all suspected it was more to do with the fact that Jas had refused to discuss taking things further with him on a physical level, and now Jas has sworn off men forever because they are all shallow scum.

'Ahem,' Tom said, when Jas reminded us that she is Over Men Because They Are Scum. 'I am here, you know.'

'She doesn't mean *you*,' I hastily assured him. 'And not Nicky either. Or Luke or Andy. Just, you know, all the others. Anyway, what positives do you think I should be focusing on then?'

Tom said I should be focusing on all my good friends, who are there for me – like him, Kate, Jas, Luke and Andy. Then he gave me a lecture about how 'This is an exciting year, Lila. You seem so intent on being miserable, you'll forget to enjoy it. This is when we plan the rest of our lives. The UCAS form you are so fixated on is our gateway to the future, not the end of the world you seem to think it is. We have so many opportunities ahead of us. Don't ruin it, for us as well as yourself, by being a moaning cow about everything!'

I opened my mouth to point out that we would blow

those opportunities if we failed our A levels, or messed up our UCAS form, but then I closed it again. Sometimes Tom's relentless positivity can be mildly irritating, but it's so rare that he's shaken out of his good-natured cool to snap at anyone, let alone rebuke them or call them a moaning cow (rude!), that I thought better of arguing with him, and agreed I would try to count my blessings.

'And it's only for a year,' Tom added. 'If you and Nicky are really meant to be, you can pick up where you left off when he comes back for university next year, can't you?'

I nodded and attempted a bright smile. All I could think was: What if he doesn't come back? What if he decides the Ohio life is for him and takes up with one of those wretched cheerleaders, who will have a cool American name like Paige or Madison, and a car, and look about twenty-five, like they all do on *Beverley Hills 90210*? Though on the plus side, if she looks twenty-five when she is seventeen, then she will probably age badly and look like a decrepit old hag by the time she actually *is* twenty-five, which would serve Nicky right.

There! See? I'm looking on the bright side already.

So yesterday I did try to be more positive about things, if only so I didn't end up making all my friends hate me, but today it's just me and Jas, and she isn't allowed to hate me, because we've been best friends since, like, *forever*, and so I find myself wallowing again. And panicking about college tomorrow and having to face the smug, sneery face of Horrible Rachel, enquiring oh so sweetly if I've heard from Nicky, and pretending to be all caring when I'm forced to admit that, so far, I have not. But he only left a week ago, and letters take a long time to cross the Atlantic.

It is not all doom and gloom, though, because after *literally* years of pleading with Mum to get the internet in the house, she finally relented, and surprised me by having it installed this week, so Nicky and I can email each other! Of course, it would have been a lot more helpful if she could have had it done a few days sooner, so Nicky could already have emailed me about how he is finding Ohio (ugh), but it was still a big step forward for Mum, who regards such modern technology with deep suspicion. In fact, poor Mum is *such* a Luddite that I had to intervene when I heard her on the phone to Aunt Lucy announcing that yes, she had *email* now, and the address? Mum sounded vague and informed Aunt Lucy that it would surely be the same as the address Aunt Lucy always used, we hadn't moved house or anything, and I had to explain to Mum that that wasn't how email worked.

Sometimes it's quite scary to think that Mum is a doctor.

Anyway. Positives. I must focus on the positives. And a

BIG positive is that Nicky *does* have my new college email address that we were all issued with at the end of last term, so hopefully when I log on in college, there will be a message from him there. With any luck, a long, devoted message about how much he loves me and how awful Ohio is and how ghastly the cheerleaders are, especially the ones called Paige and Madison!

MONDAY 8TH SEPTEMBER 1997

Oh bliss of bliss and joy of joys! There *was* an email waiting for me from Nicky! I felt a million times better for getting it, and like I could actually concentrate on college, which will probably be a great relief to Mum, who has given me a long and tedious lecture on the importance of this year, and how I mustn't let myself be distracted by boys, blah, blah, blah, etc., etc., etc.

I waited till Mr Watson, who was supervising the computer lab, had left the room and then I printed it out, along with my reply, because email is all very well, but you can't keep it, like a letter. And maybe if one day I'm a famous writer and Nicky's a famous scientist, like we both plan to be, someone will write our biographies, or maybe a joint biography – *The Couple Who Shaped the Twentieth Century*, or something like that. Except, no, the twentieth century is nearly over, we'd have to be the couple who shape the twenty-first century! That's a scary thought! I will be a Booker and Pulitzer Prize-winning Literary Great, and Nicky will probably invent something amazing that will change the world, and we will be remembered for posterity. But posterity would be better if the biographers had some material to work with.

Nicky's email was a bit shorter than I'd hoped for. And there was only one. I'd had a notion that he might have sent a tender loving message every day that he'd been gone, but he hadn't sent anything until yesterday.

But of course, I reminded myself, he would have been exhausted from travelling, and then they would need to unpack, and get the internet connected to the house, and loads of other things. Also, a message every day might have been a bit needy.

Anyway, I've stuck the messages in here, so I can read them over when I'm missing him. My reply was longer, of course, but that's because I'm going to be a writer, not a scientist like he is. It probably just means I'll get more chapters in the biography than him.

Hi Lila,

I kept typing 'dear Lila' and 'darling Lila', but that looks weird in an email. It's what you would put in a letter or a card. And then I was going to say 'you are my dear and darling Lila', but that sounds like something my granny would say, or some corny old song. I never thought I'd find it so hard to try and write down how I feel about you. It was so much easier last year, when we started college and were messaging each other anonymously through the chat room without knowing it was us. Now, I find when I am with you I can say what I want quite well, but writing it down is much harder.

Ohio is very different to England. Even the bread tastes different. Everything is bigger. Scarier. They don't have orange squash. And they really really don't understand about tea.

I miss you so much. I wish I could find the words to tell you how much I miss you. I wouldn't care about the orange squash or the tea if you were here. I started school last week. It's strange to go from feeling so grown-up at college, to being back at school. At least it's an international school, so I'm not the weird ginger British freak. Or at least, not the only one. Which makes a change.

I love you.

Nicky xx

I was a tiny bit miffed by this missive. It was all very well the 'I loves you's and the 'I miss you's, but reading this, one could be mistaken for wondering what Nicky missed more – me, or proper British beverages.

I took some heart from it, though, because I had

forgotten that Nicky wasn't going to a good old all-American high school, the sort we were so fascinated by in films. Thankfully he is going to an *international* school, as the American curriculum would have been too different for even Nicky to adapt to at this point. So HURRAH, no awful Madisons or Paiges prancing around in little cheerleading skirts! This raised my spirits immensely.

But, oh GLOOM, because who knows what harlots he might meet at an international school? There could be sexy Swedish girls, all blue eyes and wholesome charm, inviting him to go cross-country skiing with them (do they ski in Ohio? The Swedes would doubtless find a way). Then, miles from anywhere, Sexy Swedish Sonia would tumble prettily to the ground, twisting her ankle, and require Nicky to be her rescuing hero. Perhaps he would help her limp (prettily) to a woodsman's hut, where they would manage to kindle a small fire while they waited for help to find them, but they would still have to huddle together for warmth, and inevitably he would be overcome by her sexy Swedish charm and fall in love with her in a matter of moments and they would kiss passionately by the fire until the woodsman arrived to find them entwined in each other's arms, and inseparable from that moment forth! Never trust the Swedes. Look at the Vikings! Or were the Vikings Danish? Never mind, close enough. They invented IKEA anyway, which Dad says is the seventh circle of hell.

Or if not a Swedish sexpot, perhaps he would be lured by a small, dark, intensely beautiful French girl in a black polo neck and beret, blowing clouds of Gauloises smoke and quoting Simone de Beauvoir at him until he was entranced by her intellect and quirky charm and forgot me forever. This one would be particularly harsh, as I had once tried to rock the black polo neck and beret combo and everyone had asked me if I was selling onions. Or perhaps there would be a sultry Italian girl, all fire and passion and pasta? Or a sloe-eyed Spanish señorita? Or . . .

Sort yourself out, Lila. Nicky isn't like that. If there's one thing Nicky can be relied on for, it's his steadfast and true heart. He's not going to have his head turned by any foreign beauties, however prettily they may tumble in the snow, or how elegantly they may arch a Gallic eyebrow at him. Anyway, Nicky hates smoking, so Frenchy Françoise will be off the scene.

Obviously I can't tell Nicky any of these worries. He'll either think I'm quite mad, or he'll be upset I don't trust him, or he'll be yet another person telling me that I need to stop letting my imagination run away with me. So here's what I wrote to him:

Nicky! It's so so lovely to hear from you! I've sent you a letter, but I don't know how long it will take to arrive – I asked Mum to post it, and she said she wasn't paying for airmail because I hadn't used one of the special blue airmail letters on the really thin paper, so it will probably reach you sometime around the millennium, by which time we will be old and grey!

Back at college today – it's so weird without you, but Jas and Kate and Tom are here, and Luke and Andy. And Horrible Rachel, of course, who was asking after you for some reason. She's no less horrible than she was last term. I wish it was Rachel who had gone to Ohio, not you. I miss you too – so, so much! I never realised how much I was just used to you always being there next door, and now you're not, and I'm sad.

Everything else at college is just the same – Mr Lorrimer gave his speech again, and I swear it was the exact same speech he gave last year, word for word. Miss Jackson has left, but they've replaced her with another pastoral deputy head who looks and sounds exactly like her, so you'd never know she had gone. Apart from that, there's no gossip yet, or none you don't already know – except there is a new boy called Ben. He's in my French class, and everyone is already calling him Beautiful Ben because he is awfully good-looking. Horrible Rachel couldn't stop staring at him! He's too good for her, though. Everyone is too good for her, except sleazy Mark.

Anyway, free period is nearly up, so I need to go! Please email or write or something again soon, I love you too!

Lila xxx

Once I'd sent the email, I read it again, and realised it was perhaps not quite the stuff of posterity. Never mind, it isn't like the biographers will quote every word we write. Will they?

Anyway, it was probably a better effort than Nicky complaining about the lack of orange squash. Though I did wonder afterwards if it had been entirely tactful of me to mention how good-looking the new boy Ben is? Of course, he is of no interest to me, for my heart belongs to Nicky, but I should have been clearer that I only mentioned him in the hope he would be impervious to Rachel's charms and with luck bring her down a peg or two. Surely a guy as gorgeous as Ben should be destined for someone better than Rachel, who *thinks* she is stunning but is actually quite average, which wouldn't matter if she was a nice person but she really isn't – she just thinks she's so *superior*, prancing about telling everyone how her dad is a Top Lawyer, and she, Rachel, is definitely going to do Law at Cambridge because Daddy says there's no way they would turn down someone like her, and then she sneers at Jas and me because we were all at school together, where Rachel considered herself the most popular girl in the school and Jas and me to be pathetic rejects. The fact that the tables seem to have turned, and Jas and I and Nicky inexplicably became part of the popular crowd when Kate and Tom (who manage to be super-popular people but also *nice*, proving that the two things are not mutually exclusive) made friends with us instead of Rachel, has in no way stopped Rachel looking down her nose at us. So she definitely doesn't deserve Ben.

Thinking about who Ben might end up going out with has given me an idea, though. If I am to languish lovelorn and alone while Nicky dehydrates on the other side of the world for lack of orange squash, then I should throw myself into Good Works –starting with sorting out my friends' disastrous lives. After all, it was good enough for Emma Woodhouse in *Emma*, and indeed for Cher in *Clueless*, even if that was just an updated version of Emma (though *weird* that Cher ended up getting with her stepbrother. I could have understood it if the actual Emma had had to marry some dodgy relation – they were always having to marry cousins and whatnot because they would cause scandal if they ventured too far – but surely there would have been more choice available to Cher with the whole of LA to pick from). Of course, I'm doing it the wrong way round, as I have already found The One, but it would be very apt, given that before he kissed me for the very first time last

Christmas, Nicky had quoted *Emma* to me – Mr Knightley saying, 'If I loved you less, I might be able to talk about it more.' Perhaps that is why he mostly wittered on about squash in his email, because he loves me too much to talk much about it? Yes, I expect that is it.

I wonder if I should tell him of my grand plan to matchmake all our friends, or if I shall just reveal it as a *fait accompli* when I have finished and everyone is living happily ever after (except Rachel, I'm not helping her find true love, I hope she dies a lonely old embittered spinster, in a dingy basement flat, without so much as a spider plant for company, and it would serve her right for always being so very smug and annoying)?

I have decided not to tell Nicky what I am doing just yet. I suspect he might say that I'm interfering and to let people find their own ways in life without trying to meddle. He has suggested before that I can be a little overenthusiastic when I have a Very Good Idea about something – whereas I call it striking while the iron is hot.

I will wait until he finally comes home, and surprise him with everyone being deliriously happy and in love, and then I shall inform him that it's all down to *me*! And maybe, if it doesn't work out being a Literary Novelist, instead I could be an agony aunt for *Cosmopolitan* and dispense wise advice to those less fortunate than me. I would be a cool agony aunt, though, not one like Claire Rayner, and I definitely wouldn't advertise sanitary pads on TV! It's important to have options, as Mum is always telling me. I'm not sure I can put any of those potential future careers in my personal statement on my UCAS form, though.

EMILY

CHAPTER THREE

Lila really was *very* dramatic about everything! I shall remind Mum about that the next time she rolls her eyes and says, 'Oh, Emily, stop being such a *drama queen.*' Then, I will point out that a) I have *nothing,* nothing *at all* on her teenage drama, and b) if I am being slightly overdramatic, who is to blame for that? Clearly it's genetic, and given I am descended from possibly the most dramatic teenager of the nineties, then who can be surprised if sometimes I overreact slightly?

I decided that Dad must be off the phone to Stella by now, talking about how *tricky* I am. HA! Be glad you didn't have to parent Lila and her existential despair, I thought. Though I suppose he did *marry* her, so he may have some idea what Lila could be like. But surely by the time she was doing grown-up, adult things, like getting married and having a baby, she must've got the worst of it out of her system? However, Mum can still be a bit much sometimes, like when she's got a deadline looming – *not* thankfully for a sex and dating column, ugh, can you *imagine* the CRINGE if your mum was writing about *sex* in the media? That would *literally* be the worst thing in the world. I'm already worried that this novel she has written might have sex scenes in it, and my friends might read it and then how will I ever live it down?

I think I liked it better when she was writing columns about cleaning tips and life hacks and celebrity style. Not that Mum knows anything about style, she has three shops she buys clothes from, on repeat. She can't even begin to grasp the concept of TikTok Shop or Vinted or Depop. Though I must give her some credit for having the dignity to shop from places like Boden (even if it's boring), and so at least dressing like a mum. When Olivia Jones's mum split up from her dad last year, her mum got a twenty-three-year-old boyfriend and started borrowing Olivia's clothes and, worse, trying to hang out with her, *while wearing Olivia's clothes*, and asking her to teach her about contouring and stuff.

We were all mortified for Olivia.

I made Mum promise she would never do that, but she just gave me a lecture about feminism, and why shouldn't Annie Jones dress how she wanted, and there was no such thing as 'too old' for any clothes, and brainwashing women into dressing 'age appropriately' was just another tool of the patriarchy to oppress us.

Which obviously I agree with in principle.

But agreeing the patriarchy is bad and we should dismantle its outdated perceptions of how women should dress is one thing. Seeing your mother prancing out the door in a boob tube and your new sequinned Shein mini skirt before you've even had a chance to wear it yourself is quite another.

I wonder if Granny MacKay used to tell Lila she would catch a chill on her kidneys if she went out like that, like Mum does with me? Or if she let her experiment and find her own happy medium? I can't see Granny being very interested in clothes, to be perfectly honest. Even when she dresses up for a special occasion, she still just looks like she's wearing a slightly fancier version of what she wears every day.

I asked Mum about this once and got another feminism lecture on how not everyone cares about hair and clothes and make-up. For some of us, clothing is simply a functional way to stay warm and dry, nothing more, and actually more of us should make an effort to embrace that attitude instead of wasting valuable patriarchy-smashing time worrying about what we are wearing. Which once again is deeply hypocritical of Mum, because even though she only shops in old people's shops that I wouldn't be seen *dead* in, she is always fussing about her clothes and how she looks. Especially when she is going on a date and pretends it isn't a date because she doesn't want me to know she's dating, even though I can quite clearly tell when she is going on a date, and when she is just meeting friends for a drink.

Sometimes I fear my mother is not quite the feminist icon she aspires to be.

I tiptoed downstairs to get my phone, listening carefully to make sure there were no more conversations going on about me, but all was quiet. When I went into the kitchen, Dad made a big deal of being very jovial and pretending the earlier scene had never happened. I suspect this was as much to stop me asking any more awkward questions about Stella as it was to cheer me up, but he suggested we could have some ice cream and watch TV, and I thought I should probably make an effort too, if I am going to be here all summer, if only to make sure he buys us proper ice cream and doesn't make me eat Stella's 'ice cream' which she makes with aquafaba and cacao and no sugar, and tastes like very sad farts.

We settled down with a tub of Ben and Jerry's and two spoons and stuck on Netflix. Dad suggested I perhaps did not need to mention the Ben and Jerry's to Stella. I couldn't concentrate, though, because Dad does not approve of being on your phone or messaging people while you're watching TV (he calls it 'doom scrolling', even though that is not what doom scrolling is, but he feels important for knowing a word like that), but I wanted to check in with Poppy and see what was happening at home.

Part of me thought that was silly, the whole point of spending the summer with Dad was to get *away* from what was happening at home. But part of me needed to know what was going on – if Poppy had heard whether Oli and Grace had got together at Alexa Neville's party last night – which obviously we had not gone to – and if they were now strutting around town like some kind of *mature* power couple, because she is so much more grown-up than me, and Oli *deserves* someone like her. Deserves. Ha!

I realised I had snorted out loud in disgust, and Dad was looking at me oddly.

'Did you choke on the ice cream, Emily?' he asked.

'No, no . . . but actually I'm a bit tired,' I improvised. 'Travelling, and all that.'

I scraped the last spoonful of ice cream into my mouth and said my goodnights. Poor Dad obviously felt he was failing in his paternal duties, though, because as I went out the door, he said yet *again*, 'You know you can talk to me, Emily, if you want to, about anything?'

'Yeah, I know. Thanks, Dad. But I just want to go to bed, OK?'

Poppy at least messaged back that she had heard that Alexa's party had apparently been awful and her mum and dad were there the whole time and her mum actually tried to make everyone play party games, which cheered me up a bit. Poppy also said that none of Oli's year had bothered with Alexa's party, so no news about him and Grace.

Now that at least I knew Alexa's party had been rubbish and there was no confirmation about Grace and Oli, I decided that I needed to try and move on. Perhaps Lila and her matchmaking plans for her friends would have some tips for me on how to get a boyfriend who isn't after only one thing and doesn't dump you midway through the summer disco because his brains, such as they are, are clearly located in his trousers!

LILA

CHAPTER FOUR

TUESDAY 9TH SEPTEMBER 1997

Ben was obviously key to my matchmaking plan. Whether he would do for Kate or Jas or Tom was yet to be made clear, but obviously the first thing to do was to establish whether or not he was a nice enough person for any of them. I would not be a good friend if I set them up with another pig, like Mark turned out to be – not that I could be blamed there, Jas had one hundred per cent got into that herself. But if I *was* going to be responsible for their true love match, I had better make sure they were suitable.

What should be done if I found him to have major character defects? There was, of course, the option of just leaving Ben out of my plans and letting Rachel have her wicked way. Because Rachel is shallow and lacks soul, she wouldn't care if Ben was a terrible person, she'd just be all gloaty because she had snared the best-looking boy in the college. (Tom looked a little put out when he heard people referring to Ben as the best-looking boy in the college and said, slightly petulantly, that he thought we'd said *he* was the best-looking boy there. And then we had to soothe Tom's ruffled feathers by assuring him that he definitely was, but Ben was the best-looking potentially straight guy. I'm not sure he fell for it, but he concurred that that was fair. He also insisted that Ben was definitely straight, and his gaydar never failed him – that was how he and Giles had found each other. So at least it answered one of my questions about Ben.)

I wondered how to discreetly find the answer to the other burning question – about his actual personality, as opposed to his delicious dark hair and piercing blue eyes (NOT that I cared about such things, obviously, because blue eyes and almost black hair are not a patch on auburn hair and sea-green eyes). To my utter astonishment, because generally she seemed to go out of her way to make my life miserable, our French teacher Mrs Carruthers provided the opportunity by rearranging the classroom, sitting Ben beside me and announcing our partners for all our speaking exercises would now be whoever we were sharing a desk with!

Hurrah for Mrs Carruthers! Now I could ask leading questions and befriend him under the guise of French practice!

Rachel, who had been paired with Eddie Maitland, a loud and obnoxious boy who has made farting into a performance art, was livid. Especially when Eddie loudly cracked one out and shouted, *'Arrête de péter, Rachel, c'est dégoutant, ça pue, Rach!'* while flapping his hands and wafting the stench back at Rachel.

Poor Rachel. Karma is a bitch. Rachel started screaming that Eddie was lying, she hadn't farted and *he* was the disgusting one who had made the stink, then demanding Mrs Carruthers eject Eddie and give Rachel a new desk partner.

Mrs Carruthers sighed, looked up from her notebook (she had dropped it beside me when she was walking past, which is how I knew what was preoccupying her – that the salmon en croûte for her dinner party tomorrow night would not make itself), and told Rachel she needed to grow up, and also did she need to visit *les toilettes* if she was experiencing *troubles intestinaux*?

Rachel shrieked even harder at the idea that Mrs Carruthers thought she, Rachel, a delicate flower who denied possessing any bodily functions ever, let alone farting publicly, was responsible for the smell, which was pretty bad. (What on earth has Eddie been eating?)

Mrs Carruthers just turned back to her notebook, murmuring, *'C'est tout à fait naturel, Rachel,'* though her nose then twitched, and she pointed to Robbie Ellis by the window and said, *'Ouvre la fenêtre, s'il vous plaît, Robert.'* We were all quite relieved about this.

Rachel finally subsided into a furious sulky silence, casting death stares at Mrs Carruthers and Eddie, and also at me, for snaring Ben as my partner. Though Rachel's default setting with me is death stares, so I'm quite accustomed to it. I turned to Ben and opened the conversation with a casual, *'Bonjour, Ben! Qu'est-ce que vous aimes faire le weekend?'*

Ben looked blank for a moment, then announced, *'Le weekend, j'aime aller à la bibliothèque, et j'aime lire des livres. Aussi, j'aime faire du sports!'*

Very helpful, Ben. Very helpful indeed. 'I like to go to the library and I like to read books and also I like to play sports.' How am I to glean the inner nuances of your soul from that? Still, the library and reading was good. Kate and Jas might be into that. The sports less so, my friends and I are not very sporty – in fact, Tom briefly walking out with Giles the rugby captain was about as close to being sporty as any of us got. Nonetheless, I persevered and enquired what sort of sports Ben liked to play. There was another blank stare, and then Ben triumphantly offered, *'Le tennis!'*

Well, tennis was quite a civilised sport, if one must indulge in such things. Not like horrible hockey, which was surely invented as some form of torture for schoolgirls –

why else would anyone think it a good idea to arm twenty-two girls with big sticks and make the aim of the game chasing each other around a muddy field? Mrs Fitzwilliam, our old games teacher, insisted that was not the purpose of the game at all – the point was to get the ball and score goals – but you do that by *chasing people with sticks*! It's barbaric! I subscribed far more to Flora Poste's view in *Cold Comfort Farm* on such things and made a point of running away from the ball and the terrifying stick-wielding Amazons pursuing it. 'Not a team player,' Mrs Fitzwilliam wrote in my report each term, which was quite unfair as there were a lot of things I would have been happy to do in a team, just not teams that involved being pursued by your classmates with blunt objects to beat your shins with!

Rachel was captain of the A team, which tells you everything you need to know about Rachel.

I was still thinking about hockey when I realised Ben had asked me something and was now staring at me expectantly. I asked if he could repeat it and earned a stern look from Mrs Carruthers. I had better pull my socks up, I don't want her moving me away from Ben and sitting me with Stinky Eddie Fartface instead. Oh, he was wanting to know if I liked sports.

I gave a firm, '*NON*,' before informing him I preferred reading.

Ben laughed and said, *'Moi aussi,'* which was promising. So I asked him what he liked to read, and he said, *'Livres sur les trains,'* which seemed slightly peculiar, but we persevered to have a slightly stilted discussion about books, which to be honest was somewhat beyond either of our vocabularies, and apart from books about trains, he seemed to like some other very odd kinds of books, but at least Mrs Carruthers was satisfied we were talking about *something*.

The lesson finally ended, to everyone's relief (the stench Eddie had unleashed on the classroom had never entirely dissipated), and we all sloped off to lunch. Ben fell into step beside me. I could actually feel the burning between my shoulder blades from Rachel's furious glare.

Ben apologised for talking a load of nonsense and said he seemed to have forgotten most of his French over the summer and had only understood about half of what we'd been saying.

This was too much for Rachel to let pass, and she barged in to the conversation.

She started simpering on at Ben about how if you don't use a language, you *do* forget it very quickly, but luckily for *Rachel* ('I'm Rachel, by the way,' she'd said coyly, fluttering her lashes at Ben – I don't think I was quite sure until then what anyone looked like when they were either being coy or fluttering their lashes. It's not the best look, tbh), she had spent the summer in France, at one of Daddy's clients' villas ('Daddy's a lawyer, actually' – oh, do bore off, Rachel, are you going to shoehorn Daddy being a lawyer into every single conversation?). Ben made vague noises about how that must've been nice, while Rachel blithely informed him that she was *so fluent* she could probably sit the exam *right now* and get an A. Eddie passed us and gave a sarcastic snort at this.

Undaunted, Rachel then proceeded to offer Ben some catch-up lessons, because, you know, she's *so fluent*.

There seemed to be a big difference between what Ben actually said, which was to mumble something about that was very kind and certainly he'd bear that in mind, and what Ben's eyes said, which was a sort of haunted 'I can't think of anything worse'.

Rachel, though, being incredibly thick-skinned, did not realise Ben was attempting to gently decline her somewhat pushy offer, and then suggested if he sat with her at lunch, they could start straight away!

Poor Ben, the haunted look was replaced by a bunny-in-the-headlights gaze of terror, as he blinked hard and then said, 'Oh, thanks, but maybe some other time, because I was going to sit with –'

He stared at me for a moment, clearly having completely forgotten my name, and I held up my French folder behind Rachel's back, with 'Lila MacKay' clearly written over the front.

Ben wiped the sweat from his brow and finished, '– with LILA!' He then made matters worse by calling Rachel 'Rebecca' and she had to remind him what her name was.

I fear none of this will be easily forgiven. It was bad enough that last year I'd accidently found myself sitting with Kate and Tom at lunch on the first day, and that was how we all ended up becoming such good friends. And now, one day into the new term, I had annexed Beautiful Ben. There is an excellent chance that Rachel will poison my tuna baked potato in revenge. It would almost be worth it, just for the impotent rage and disbelief on her face before she stormed off. Almost.

Ben gave me a relieved smile, and thanked me for rescuing him, and then added that I didn't need to feel obliged to sit with him, he just didn't know anyone else's name yet.

I assured him that that was quite all right, and he was more than welcome to join my friends and me. I was careful to stress that this would be a group setting, not an intimate *déjeuner à deux*, lest he think I was throwing myself at him as blatantly as Rachel had. I also thought, just to be on the safe side (though it was highly unlikely

Ben would fancy *me*), I had better try to remember to make a few casual mentions of my boyfriend. But not too many, in case he thought I was just some mad fantasist who had invented a boyfriend in Ohio because I was too sad and lonely and desperate to get a real boyfriend.

Oh, *why* had Nicky gone to Ohio and made life so *complicated*?

Ben seemed to get on well with everyone at lunch, though, which was obviously a big help in my cunning plan of setting him up with Jas or Kate. All in all, it was a perfectly pleasant lunchtime, and Ben seemed entirely normal, even explaining away his strange book subject choice in French class as his mind going blank of any other suitable words, hence why he had informed me he liked books about trains. He also confessed he didn't really like tennis that much; again, he had just been trying to think of another hobby, and every word of French he had painstakingly learned over the years had fled from his mind with nerves at starting a new sixth-form college where he didn't know anyone.

He had moved here from Wales, because his parents had split up and his mother wanted to move closer to her parents. And his dad works away on the oil rigs in the North Sea, so he couldn't continue living with him.

'And I was absolutely terrified, and I was too shy to talk

to anybody yesterday, so although I was *awful* at that French speaking, I was quite glad of it, just to have someone to talk to,' Ben admitted.

How can someone as gorgeous as Ben be anxious about talking to people? I just assumed he would have been mobbed with people trying to befriend him, rather than me being the first person apart from teachers that he'd actually spoken to, and then only under duress because Mrs Carruthers made me.

Maybe, like Tom, he is so used to how he looks that he has no idea of how attractive he actually is – except Tom, outwardly anyway, is very outgoing and confident. It's only when you really get to know him that you realise it's mostly bravado to cover up his many insecurities. And while Ben does seem genuinely quiet and shy, he also seems very nice – I like him!

EMILY

CHAPTER FIVE

Today, even though it is my first proper day here, and it is the *summer holidays*, Dad dragged me into work with him, saying he didn't want me to sit around moping on my own all day. Moping! How unfair.

At the university, he found me various incredibly boring jobs to do, like photocopying. Who even photocopies things any more? It was all a pointless waste of time, not to mention paper. I pointed out the environmental effects of this, and said did he *want* to kill the polar bears, but he said he didn't think half a dozen sheets of paper were really going to tip the climate crisis over the edge. I said yes, but what if everyone thought like that, but Dad just sighed and told me to get on with it. He kept me so busy that I didn't even have time to message Poppy till I was graciously permitted a lunchbreak. But Poppy didn't reply, which sent me into a panic about what she was doing without me. I convinced myself that she was probably having too much fun to bother with me, and my *moping*. Perhaps, I fretted, she was double dating with Oli and Grace and no longer had time for such a *moping loser* as me.

To my relief, my phoned finally pinged when I trudged through the front door after Dad, exhausted by being forced to work my fingers to the bone all day. Surely there are laws against such child labour? Dad said I was being dramatic and if I thought a bit of light photocopying was hard work, wait till I discovered what *real* work involved.

I dashed upstairs to open the message before Dad starting on about 'doom scrolling' again, and as I had hoped, it was from Poppy! Yay! What's happening at home?

Yo how's Surrey so boring here without u

have joined the theatre summer school like Mum said I had to.

She still said I had to do something apart from watching TikToks

even though they are about SCIENCE so EDUCATIONAL

my fave was a really interesting one on the science behind opening a jar apparently doing a TOUR

gonna try and get tickets

yes I know u think science TikToks are BORING but yolo

Poppy had been utterly obsessed by this science TikTokker recently, and her latest career plan, having gone through hairdresser, influencer, the next Taylor Swift, psychologist and fashion designer, was to become a scientist. She was a little vague on what sort of scientist, but she spent hours watching these TikToks and sending them to me with instructions as to why they were interesting. In fairness, despite myself, they *were* interesting. The TikTokker had a way of making even boring things sound fun and explaining them really well, so you understood the actual science. If only our teachers could do the same. The texts from Poppy kept coming though.

Guess who else is at the theatre school lol

grace walker

haven't seen oli but grace seems really nice

I was stunned and outraged by such a betrayal from Poppy, so I immediately messaged her back, so furious that it was only semi-intelligible due to autocorrect.

Pops what u think u doing

u can't be friends with Grace

Grace stole Oli!

Ems, she didn't steal him

u can't steal people

she hasn't mentioned him anyway

prob they not even together

I jus said she was nice was all

Can't believe u are doing this!

I'm not doing anything

u went away for the summer

I can have other friends!!!!!!!

We went back and forth like this for a while, with many passive-aggressive full stops and exclamation marks thrown in for good measure, even though Mum says she's never heard anything so ridiculous as full stops being 'passive aggressive', until Poppy sent a text that just said

U r being silly now.

And before I could think, I replied

I am NOT.

I h8 u.

I flung my phone across the room in rage. How *dare* Poppy first get all cosy with man-stealing Grace Walker and then tell me I was being *silly* for getting mad? What does Poppy know anyway? She's never even had a boyfriend; she has no idea how I am feeling. No one does.

Even Lila wouldn't have understood. What was Mum thinking, giving me that diary to read to make me feel better? It was supposed to be about Lila's own heartbreak, and instead it's all about her being melodramatic and self-pitying, not *heartbroken* and certainly not humiliated. Being a bit miserable and missing your boyfriend because he's moved to another country is not *at all* the same as what happened to me, or what I'm feeling!

And don't even start me on how wretched it feels to have Poppy, *Poppy* of all people, betray me with slutty Grace Walker. You're not meant to slut-shame, I know, but why should I be nice about Grace? Despite Poppy saying Grace hasn't mentioned Oli, as far as I am concerned, she's taken my boyfriend, and now she's stolen my best friend, and she's *totally* ruined my summer, and stupid feminism says I can't even call her slutty. It's just not fair.

I huffed around my bedroom a bit more, and decided to read some more of Lila's whiny diary, if only so that tomorrow I could call Mum and tell her that it had been entirely pointless giving it to me, and that it showed a huge lack of self-awareness on her part, and that there were clearly no similarities between our situations. That would show her!

LILA

CHAPTER SIX

SATURDAY 20TH SEPTEMBER 1997

Finally, finally, a letter from Nicky!

I haven't been able to print out and save our emails, because college is 'economising' and so Mr Watson guards the printer like a dragon does its hoard. To be honest, the emails have mostly been Nicky talking about settling in and what he's doing at school and what exotic fast food we know not of here that he has sampled now (Taco Bell! Wendy's! What's wrong with a Wimpy?). Try as I might to read between the lines, it's been a struggle to find the romance. So I had much higher hopes when the long-anticipated Actual Letter arrived.

Dear Lila,

I'm not sure what the point of this letter is, as we'll probably have sent loads of emails by the time you even get it, so I'll have told you all my news, but you said you wanted letters, so here is a letter.

The flight here was OK. The film was good – it was the new Jurassic Park. And the meal was chicken in some sort of sauce. I didn't like the sauce, but there was a bread roll, and chocolate mousse for pudding.

The house that Dad's company found for us is nice. The internet is not connected yet, so I'll email you when it is. We have a tumble drier. Mum said it's a waste of electricity and hung the laundry out in the garden like usual and all the neighbours were really surprised as apparently people don't do that here.

It is true what people say about everything being much bigger here. I feel very small sometimes. I went to the 'mall' with Mum this morning, and we got lost in it and couldn't find our way out. I thought perhaps that would be the rest of my life now, wandering the halls of the giant mall, having to live there, scavenging leftovers from the food court at night, until we evolved into some sort of mall-based mutant subspecies, unable to go outside in daylight or digest anything but processed sugar, and I would never see you again, and maybe one day, in a thousand years, the remains of the Mall Rats civilisation would be found, in the levels beneath Gap and Macy's, and written on the walls would be poems to Lila, the lost love of the Mall Rats king. But we did find our *way out, so hopefully I will see you again, and not in a thousand years.*

I miss you so much,

Love,

Nicky

Well, as letters go, I had mixed feelings.

Initially, it was very disappointing – the talk of how he wasn't sure of the point in writing to me, then all the guff about the food on the plane and his mother's laundry. I suppose, if you look beyond Nicky becoming some mutant rat king, there was some romance to be found in his vision of poems to me being found in a thousand years because his love for me is so enduring. It just would've been nicer if he had envisaged them carved into rocks fifty metres high, like that valley where they sculpt the presidents' faces, instead of scratched behind the central heating pipes by a scuttling malformed rodent man fleeing the cruel bright light to hide in the darkness forever.

But I suppose one can't have everything.

I immediately sat down and wrote him a reply, of course. As he had predicted, there wasn't a lot that I hadn't already told him in the emails (the emails haven't been as frequent as I had hoped, and I usually feel that once I've sent him one, I can't send another until he replies, and sometimes he takes several days to do that, which does not particularly seem the act of someone aflame with undying passion), but I told him all about college yesterday, which wasn't that interesting, and Kate's start-of-term party last night, which was a week later than last year because last Friday was her dad's birthday.

Having spent ages writing the letter, I can't be bothered copying it all out here, so I think I'll just stick his letters in, and if our biographers want a full record of our correspondence, Nicky will have to provide my letters. Assuming he keeps them. That's what you do with letters, isn't it? Especially love letters, which surely these are? You tie them up with a red ribbon that fades over time, and one day your grandchildren find them in the attic and marvel at how this otherworldly love still burns on the page with as much desire as it did one hundred years ago, because that's how passionate you both were about each other. Everyone knows that. It's practically the *law*!

Anyway, it was a very good party. Since Kate's dad Kevin is insanely rich, and Kate and Kevin live in an *actual* mansion with an *actual* swimming pool, and since Kevin is always very generous about getting drinks and food for Kate's friends, parties at Kate's house are usually brilliant and this one was no exception.

Kate had invited 'the gang' – Tom, Jas, Andy, Luke and

me – to come early to get everything ready. There wasn't much to do, really. We set out all the drinks, and nodded politely as Kevin reminded us that things were 'not to get out of hand', then he went off to his golf club for the evening, leaving Kate an enormous sum of money to order pizzas for everyone.

I wonder what it must be like to be so hugely rich that you never have to think about money. We aren't *poor*, of course – but even if Mum and Dad hadn't got divorced, and Dad hadn't taken up with my ghastly stepmother Anita, who cares only for her Border terriers, we still wouldn't be even *close* to the sort of richness that Kate and Kevin are.

Naturally, they would both tell you that money can't buy happiness. Mum said this was a very shallow outlook and there were other ways to be rich than just in money. Which is exactly the sort of thing adults always say when they're trying to be clever and remind you how much wiser they are than you, like we know *nothing*, just because we're teenagers, so our emotions are somehow less valid than theirs.

Why should that be? Why are Mum and Dad's views and opinions and feelings about things considered so much more important than mine? All right, maybe I don't have as much experience of the world, and of course they've done things and seen things that I haven't yet – like getting married and having a child. But that doesn't mean they just get to be right about everything all the time.

And when does it stop? If *I* get married and have a baby, will they then acknowledge that maybe at last I'm as mature as they are, and know something about the world, or will they just be all like, 'Oh, Lila! You can't possibly understand, you must wait until you're a grandparent.'

If ever I *do* have a baby and that baby grows up and dares to think for him or herself, I will not squash their feelings and tell them that they don't know what real life is like. I will listen and I will understand and I will remember what it is like to be a child or a teenager.

I wish I could articulate all these things to Nicky when we write or email, but they sound so pretentious when I write them down. Also, talking about our future children might freak him out a tiny bit – I'm not sure he would understand that I mean it from a purely hypothetical point of view.

I think I would do far better at parenting than Mum and Dad. To be perfectly honest, out of the responsible adults in my life, Anita is probably the one with the most parental instincts, though she channels them all into her Border terriers. She called them her 'babies' once, and I saw an expression cross Dad's face suggesting that he wondered what he'd done, marrying her. Not that I want my tummy tickled and to be called Mrs Snufflebumpkin, of course.

Anyway. I had thought I would spend the whole party either moping and missing Nicky, or feeling abject mortification at how at Kate's start-of-term party last year I had foolishly thrown myself at Tom. But as it turned out, I neither moped nor was mortified – well, no more than usual, anyway.

The party was just starting to get going when the huge pile of pizzas Kate had ordered from Domino's arrived. (Oh, the luxury! Mum sniffs at Domino's as overpriced American rubbish and refuses to countenance the decadence of ordering a pizza to be delivered.) The boys fell on the pizzas like starving wolves. The girls hung back and tried to look a little more decorous and hoped the greedy-pig boys wouldn't wolf the lot before we got a chance to grab a slice in a ladylike way. Then it occurred to me that there was no one to impress with my delicate table manners anyway, so I elbowed the boys out the way and grabbed myself a large slab of delicious pizza and took a huge bite.

Alas, such greed was not to go unpunished. In the scrum I had inadvertently snatched a slice covered in the kryptonite of lovely pizza – PINEAPPLE.

I was just wondering how and where to discreetly spit out the devil fruit when in sashayed Rachel, looking as smug as it is possible for a human being to look without exploding into a cloud of flying fragments of smugness. A sheepish-looking Ben was trailing in her wake.

Bloody, *bloody* Rachel.

There had been much debate about whether to invite her, and eventually Kate, who is a kinder and nicer soul than me, said she didn't really see how she could invite everyone else we knew, and *not* Rachel, even if she is a holy terror, as sadly she is friends with too many of the other people who were coming.

I use the term 'friends' loosely. I don't believe Rachel has any *real* friends that she truly likes, just people she is nice to because she feels like they can be useful to her or improve her social standing.

When I said this to Kate, she said that maybe I should try and see the best in people, instead of the worst. This is easy for Kate to say, though, when she has only known Rachel a year. If she had known her for as long as Jas and I have, she would know that there is no better nature to Rachel.

Jas and I did a quiz in *Cosmo* over the summer about 'Are Your Friends Psychos?' and we answered it with Rachel in mind, and according to *Cosmo,* Rachel is almost certainly a sociopath. I'm not entirely sure what that is, or if it's better or worse than a psychopath, but it's definitely not good. Despite this, Kate insisted that Rachel could not be excluded from the party on the basis of a magazine quiz of dubious scientific merit.

And so here she was, and here was Beautiful Ben, who must've given in to her charms in the end. (I will grant that Rachel is not *un*attractive, if one is able to look past her major character flaws, and in the spirit of being entirely fair, at least some of my dislike of her *might* stem from what shiny, swishy hair she has – a bit like Jennifer Aniston's!) And here was I, with a mouthful of half-chewed pineapple pizza, and a gag reflex threatening to kick in at any moment.

Ben waved across the kitchen at me, and I decided that swallowing the pineapple was the lesser of the evils on offer, given the option was now spitting it out, soggy and slabbery, on to Rachel's brand-new pink Adidas trainers in front of everyone. That would be a hard one to recover from. I gulped bravely as Ben came over, immediately followed by Rachel, who fixed me with a beady glare as Ben said, '*Bonjour*, Lila!'

Rachel clutched his arm possessively and swished that stupidly swishy hair. How was it even shinier? How? Why can't she be a nice enough person that I could ask what conditioner she uses so that I too can have shiny, swishy hair? She trilled, 'Oh, Ben! I think we've done enough French practice for now, don't you? If you know what I mean, Lila!'

This last was delivered to me in a hiss that would have made Eve think twice about an apple crumble. Even I, accustomed to Rachel's snide asides and contemptuous put-downs, was taken aback by the venom in her voice. She dragged Ben away, demanding he find her a drink, because apparently the responsibility of having PERFECT HAIR means you can't open a can of Budweiser yourself, and I sighed, as it seemed I had swallowed the pineapple for nothing, and Rachel had thwarted my plans for Ben.

It was inevitable that my run of luck as the thwarter of Rachel rather than the thwartee would come to an end eventually. From the day we started college, Rachel has been enraged by what she perceived as me taking her true place with the popular people. And then, when Nicky won a prestigious photography competition, with photos of *me* of all people, and had his ugly duckling transformation from college geek to local star, Rachel had tried to throw herself at him, but again got the brush-off in favour of me. So really, it was too much to hope that fate would also snatch Ben from her impeccably flossed and expensively orthodontised jaws and toss him into my lap to dance like a puppet to my plans for him. Even though my plans were not for myself, but rather for the future happiness and companionship of my dearest friends. I had to let her have this one.

It could be worse. Maybe Ben really *was* massively into books about trains and now Rachel would have to endure many fascinating conversations about locomotive engines. That would be quite funny, actually. Ben could be the most interesting or the most boring person in the world, and Rachel would still hang in there just because she liked the way dating a sixth form college version of Brad Pitt made *her* look.

I returned to the pizza, shoving Andy out the way yet again ('Seven!' he said proudly when I asked him how many slices he had eaten so far). Selecting a slice with more care this time, I was rewarded with delicious, fruit-free pepperoni.

Andy is a very nice boy, even if he's someone none of us think of romantically. He's one of those people who's just always sort of there in the background. But he is kind, and reliable, and funny and good-natured, and I could think of many worse ways to spend my evening than chatting to Andy and eating pizza. And I'm sure, one day, there will be some sweet and lovely girl who *will* look at Andy and think, 'Yes! He is my One!' Because surely there is someone for everyone out there? Even Rachel. Maybe.

And actually there must be more than one perfect match per person, because what if there *was* only one, and that person lived in Beijing, and you lived in Birmingham, and the chances of you meeting were infinitesimally small? Hardly anyone would live happily ever after!

It occurs to me that this is a very profound thought, and I should definitely put it in my next letter to Nicky, so I sound clever and philosophical. That is one of the downsides of going out with Nicky – he is so desperately clever about everything, and just seems to *know* things, that sometimes I feel quite stupid when he starts talking about something and I have to just nod and smile and look like I know what he's on about. It's not so bad if he's talking about physics or chemistry or something scientific, because he knows I'm not taking any of those subjects, and they're not my strong points, so he will attempt to explain or keep it relatively simple. But when he starts on about philosophy or art or politics, he seems to assume I will be as well read and knowledgeable as he is, and quite often I find myself out of my depth.

I mean, it's nice he thinks I'm as clever as he is, obviously. But sometimes I wish we could just talk about *Neighbours* or *Home and Away*. Nicky thinks Australian soap operas are rotting the minds of our generation. I love them. I want to go surfing and tell people to 'rack off' and spend all my time in a coffee shop or diner that is clearly economically unviable given its ludicrously small customer base.

I suppose by going out with the boy next door I am achieving the soap dream of only having friends and partners from the same street, though. I suggested to Mum that I might take a gap year and go to Australia. She thought it was a great idea, until she asked what I was going to do, and I foolishly admitted my main plan was to visit the *Neighbours* and *Home and Away* locations, and she said she wasn't paying my airfare halfway round the world just for *that*. I'll have to ask Dad about it instead, and come up with some more highbrow options to see.

Though of course that plan was before Nicky went to Ohio. Do I really want to be in Australia when he comes home, and miss out on another year with him? Maybe he could come to Australia with me? I won't mention Summer Bay and Ramsay Street till we're there.

Andy, at least, is also a fan of Aussie soaps, and we were just discussing the astonishing return of Harold Bishop in *Neighbours* when Ben came over, remarkably without Rachel, who after two cans of lager had been forced to let him go while she went for a wee. Ben also turned out to be a secret *Neighbours* watcher, and so we all grabbed more pizza and a couple of beers each and made a dash for the garden. We fled down paths and round hedges, till we found the secret corner that Kate and Tom had shown us, and collapsed there, giggling. We were only just in the nick of time. Rachel had come out the house as we bolted, screeching had anyone seen Ben?

Ben put his head in his hands and groaned that Rachel had not left him alone all night. At college, he said, she was always there, offering her infernal French tuition, or to 'show him around town' or asking him to walk her to the library because she had too much to carry. For shame, Rachel, bad feminist, letting the side down by playing the weak and feeble woman! And then, apparently, she had simply told Ben he was coming to the party with her and he hadn't known how to say no, so he had agreed, but now he was terrified and begged us for suggestions on how to get away from her if she found him again.

I spotted my opportunity. Never let it be said that I do not strike while the iron is hot!

'Well, Ben,' I said brightly. 'One way to get Rachel off your back would be if you were going out with someone else. I'm sure she'd give up if you had a girlfriend. She's not going to make *that* much of a fool of herself. You just need to find someone. I'm sure that won't be hard!'

Mwahahaha! It won't be hard at all, not with Chief Matchmaker Lila on the case! On reflection, I think I will point Ben in the direction of Jas, who would benefit from getting some closure from her current Man-Hating

Phase. It would do her good to see that there were boys in the world who were nice *and* hot.

We lounged under the trees and chatted for a while longer, until someone turned the music up back at the house, and they were playing 'Disco 2000', which I love, so we scrambled up and went back to the party, Andy and I promising to protect Ben from Rachel. She'd gone home in a sulk when she couldn't find him, though, so he was quite safe.

EMILY

CHAPTER SEVEN

Oh Mother, how hypocritical thou art! Pah! Lila's so-called gloom is nothing, *nothing* to what I'm enduring. She doesn't even seem that bothered about Nicky being away any more, too busy wittering on about fancy parties and having a ball with good-looking Ben and nice-but-unfanciable Andy.

Whereas now, not only do I have the misery of Oli chucking me, I have also had a fight with Poppy, and what if she never forgives me? If Lila could be miserable over her boyfriend spending a few months in America, then I think I get to be considerably more despairing over losing my best friend *and* my boyfriend to Grace Bloody Walker.

It's clear Lila knew nothing about real unhappiness.

After dinner with Dad (pasta again! With pesto this time) and watching more TV for a while, I made my excuses about going to bed, and I tried to cheer myself up about how many things in the diary I could now use to hold over Mum. It's important to find a silver lining where you can.

It wasn't much consolation, though, not in the face of a future without Poppy in it. Was it too late to fix things?

I looked at my messages again to see how bad they were, or if there was any room to backtrack. It was actually worse when I looked at them again. There isn't really much coming back from telling your best friend you hate her, because she has perfidiously betrayed you with your over-sexed nemesis.

But of all the people Poppy could've palled up with, or chosen to tell me she was hanging out with, why did it have to be *Grace*? Couldn't she just have not mentioned her? Or not rubbed my nose in how *nice* Grace is? There is the *tiniest* chance that I *might've* overreacted, but at the same time, Poppy was very insensitive to my feelings. Next thing, she'll be best friends with horrible Alexa Neville too, just to really upset me!

Maybe coming away to Dad's wasn't such a good idea. Maybe I've just run away from the good as well as the bad, and made everything worse for myself. If I was at home, then maybe I'd be at theatre school with Poppy, and she wouldn't have had a chance to be friends with Grace, even if I'd had to see Grace prancing about being all sexy and popular and *mature*, which would have been grim.

Then again, in the general scheme of things, I'd rather stick rusty pins in my eyes than go to a theatre school, so maybe Poppy wouldn't be there either, and we'd just be having fun together, nowhere near Grace, so this is all my fault.

And if I am going to overthink things, I might as well overthink them as far as possible, so maybe Poppy will be discovered by a Hollywood agent at the theatre school and become a huge star and it will all be because of me going away and leaving her with nothing else to do, and she will be so grateful she'll buy me a mansion in LA, so we're never apart again, and we'll both live happily ever after.

Except even I, Poppy's dearest friend (at least until a few hours ago), must admit that Poppy's acting skills are limited and she's only really at theatre school because it seemed the least awful of the options offered by her mother, who said Poppy had to do *something* with her summer, and not just sit around the house scrolling TikTok while her parents were at work, and so it was theatre school or sports camp, and Poppy is even less sporty than me (and Lila. I have that much in common with my mother anyway, in that we both regard hockey as a barbaric and unnecessarily violent game). Poppy lobbied for a science camp, to further her scientific ambitions, but they were all residential and very expensive, so her parents said no, because they are not convinced Poppy's passion for science is anything but her latest fad. In fairness to her parents, I suspect she just wants to look serious and sexy in a white coat, and become a science influencer rather than some sort of dusty academic, shut in a cellar working for years on discovering an obscure molecule.

Anyway. Maybe Poppy will learn to act. Worse, maybe *Grace* will bring out Poppy's secret world-class abilities in some previously unsuspected field. Maybe somehow Grace will even unlock Poppy's scientific genius and she *will* become a famous and super-rich science influencer and it will be *Grace* she's eternally grateful to, LA mansion bought for, etc., and I will be left here, *photocopying* and *moping* and mouldering alone in suburbia like a single soggy potato that fell out of the bag and is rotting forgotten in the fridge under a cabbage.

I was so depressed at the thought of my lonely cabbage-buried-potato future that I had a huge cry until I felt so exhausted with woe that I curled up in bed to go to sleep without even brushing my teeth. What need do unloved and unwanted root vegetables have for teeth anyway? It's not like anyone is ever going to kiss me again. I have no more reasons to smile. My teeth may as well blacken and fall out. No one will care. Well, Mum will care and will lecture me, if I stop brushing and flossing, and I will never hear the end of it next time she drags me to the dentist.

Lila was never so despairing she gave up on her teeth.

I was surprised by how well I slept after all the crying. I hadn't thought I'd sleep at all, just toss and turn the night away on a storm of emotion, but one minute I was staring at the ceiling envisaging my future as a wizened toothless crone, doomed eternally to hear my mother nagging, 'I told you to brush your teeth, Emily,' and the next thing I knew it was Dad's voice outside the door saying, 'Emily are you awake? Time to get up, we need to go soon.'

For the next three endless days, Dad dragged me into his office with him. I have photocopied, I have been made to sort something called a *card index* (I still don't understand what it is), and then last night, I begged to be allowed to spend the day at home, pointing out yet again that I was *supposed* to be on *holiday,* and that it would be Friday and practically the weekend. Dad agreed that perhaps it wouldn't be the end of the world if I didn't go with him – I think he wasn't finding my contributions as useful as he had hoped, and he had been quite cross when I spilled my Diet Coke all over the card index thingy.

So I had been hopeful of a nice lie-in this morning, but Dad apparently felt he couldn't just leave me in bed and go out, so I was woken up at practically dawn yet again by him knocking on the door to tell me he was going now.

I rolled over and made a vaguely awake noise in response. I felt that should have been sufficient, and I could go back to sleep, but Dad had obviously decided to take his parenting duties seriously and rapped on the door again.

'Emily? Are you sure you'll be all right here by yourself? Or will I call Stella – she got back from the Lake District last night – and ask her to come over and keep you company?'

I sat bolt upright with horror and squawked, 'NO! NO! NO! No, I mean, I'll be fine, I don't want to bother Stella, I'm sure she'll have lots to catch up on,' before Dad could embark on having one of his 'Emily, I wish you'd just give Stella a chance' chats with me. 'I'll entertain myself; it'll be fine!'

'You won't just spend all day on your phone? I promised your mum I wouldn't let you spend all summer staring at a screen.'

'No! I'll read! Go for a walk. Maybe . . .' I felt inspired, 'I'll do some gardening!'

Dad seemed unconvinced by this, reminding me I didn't really know anything about gardening and muttering something about Stella trying to grow herbs, and not to dig them up, but in the end he seemed to decide that my list of activities was sufficiently wholesome and that I could be left to my own devices without breaking any of his promises to Mum.

Dad slammed out the front door. I decided I might as well get up, now I was thoroughly awake after the shock of being threatened with Stella babysitting me. I was already feeling babyish enough after everything that had happened without needing Stella drooping around the place trying to cheer me up with her vegan sugar-free cacao balls, which tasted like she'd dug them up out of her cat litter tray.

I shuffled around the house for a while, then decided I needed to be proactive. I had spent the past three days dejectedly checking my phone for messages from Poppy that never came, and imagining more and more dramatic scenarios of Poppy's glittering and glamourous future without me. Well, if Poppy was going to be famous, maybe so would I. Poppy could become a science influencer, but I too would become a massive TikTokker, and perhaps be even more famous than Poppy. And definitely more famous than Grace, who after all was going to be nothing but Poppy's assistant.

I tried to think of a TikTok trend that I could excel at. Not make-up, or clothes; Poppy and I had tried that, with no success. Something different. Something I could really make my own. Then it occurred to me that I'd already come up with it this morning! I would be a viral *gardening* TikTokker!

Fifteen minutes later, I had weeded some things that I now suspected might have indeed been Stella's herbs, and

I'd tried to pull up some dandelions with limited success, and then I'd tried digging a bit, but the whole thing was very sweaty and strenuous and now I was too hot, and covered in mud, and something had bitten me in an unspeakable place, so I gave up on the whole stupid idea.

There had to be easier ways to become more famous than Poppy.

I stomped inside and deleted my gardening videos. I was still hopeful every time I looked at my phone that there would be an apology from Poppy, swearing off Grace and vowing eternal devotion only to me, but there was still nothing. I wondered if I should apologise to her? After all, I was the one who'd said I hated her.

I scrolled TikTok for a bit while I thought about what to do, and then, deciding that perhaps I should try to be a better person, and that I would definitely text Poppy to apologise in a bit, I thought I could practise my 'better person' resolution by keeping my word about not spending all day on my phone (though technically I hadn't, because there had been the ill-fated gardening episode). So as I hadn't had time to look at Lila's diary for a while, I fetched it to see what she'd found to moan about next.

LILA

CHAPTER EIGHT

SATURDAY 18TH OCTOBER 1997

Arrrrgghhhh! I have had almost no time for this diary, because it's all getting very REAL now! So real! Too real! Grown-up life is very much breathing down my neck and I fear it's not the glorious breeze of freedom I'd always thought it would be, but rather it has halitosis and could use a Polo mint.

College is constantly nagging about getting our personal statements ready for our UCAS forms, and now we're going to university open days. Dad insisted I had to go and look at Edinburgh, because it's where *he* went, and so there was a long and awkward drive north with Mum and Dad and Anita and me in the car together for the first time, with Mum and Dad trying to make forced and jolly conversation with each other, while attempting to ignore the giant elephant in the car, which was that they'd met each other at medical school in Edinburgh. I think they were both afraid of making Anita sulk even more, because she hadn't been allowed to bring any of her Border terriers along for the trip, not even Mrs Snufflebumpkin, who Anita insisted *loved* a road trip.

Edinburgh was perfectly nice. But it's *so far away*. So far away from Jas, and Tom and all my other friends. So far from Mum. And Dad. And even so far away from Anita and Mrs Snufflebumpkin and co. It is literally in another country. And no one else I know is thinking of applying there.

Dad said I should stop being so wet about it, and seize the opportunity to make new friends and have a new start. I thought this was very unfair, as that is not what I'm doing at all. I just don't know if I want to be SO far away from everything I have ever known.

I am already resigned to the fact I'm going to be parted from Jas whatever happens, as she is determined to go to Oxford or Imperial College to do Chemistry. I am not interested in any of Imperial's courses (even if I was smart enough to get in), and I am *definitely* not clever enough for Oxford. Dad said this was a very defeatist attitude and I would certainly never get in to Oxford if I carried on like that. At least he has given up hope of me becoming a doctor like him and Mum, and has accepted that I will be doing some sort of arts-based course.

Part of me thinks I should apply to lots of London universities, so if Jas goes to Imperial, at least we could still be near each other. I suggested this to Tom, and he very gently said he wasn't sure that was the best criteria by which to choose a university. After all, what if Jas *didn't* go to London? He also implied that there was something a little bit sad about trailing after Jas because I'm too scared to be on my own.

I should really try to be braver. Tom is going to put English at Durham as his first choice because he feels it is sufficiently far away from his family, especially his father, who Tom is too scared to tell he's gay, so it would be a chance to finally be open about himself with people. Poor Tom. At least I don't have to worry about that. Dad is not the most empathetic person (I don't think you could be, married to Anita), but he tries to be supportive in his own way, even though he's disappointed about my life choices, or at least my refusal to consider medicine as a career. (He did not seem to think my horror of blood and general squeamishness around sick people was any sort of impediment, merely saying briskly, 'Oh, everyone feels like that, darling, you needn't worry, that's what nurses are for, to actually be nice to the patients and do the caring bit,' which explains a lot about doctors really.)

Kate is thinking about some sort of art school, though

she doesn't know where. She's the sort of person that things just go right for, though, wherever she goes and whatever she does. Perhaps it's because she's so beautiful and nice that people always gravitate towards her and want to be friends with her – a bit like Ben. Perhaps if I was more like either of them, I wouldn't be scared about having to go off to a strange city, where I don't know a soul.

And then there's Nicky.

I know, I know, it is the MOST UNFEMINIST thing in the world to even consider where your boyfriend might be going when it comes to things like university and career choices, but it would be nice if he'd give me some sort of a hint. I've asked him a few times if he's given it any thought, but his replies have got vaguer and vaguer, and I don't feel I can ask him again. In fact, he's becoming more and more noncommittal about everything. He takes days to reply to my emails, and they're getting shorter when he does finally send one. And there has only been one other letter since the first one. At this rate, I'm not going to need a very long piece of faded red ribbon to tie these letters up with.

I don't really feel I can nag him about letters, though. It's a bit desperate. Instead, I try and seem as jolly and positive and enthusiastic about things as I can in my emails. I tell him what's happening at college, who's going out with who, what we did in class, the parties we go to and what goes on at them. I'm doing my very best to make him feel like he's here with us, and not missing out. I sometimes wonder why I bother, though. He tells me almost nothing about what's going on in his life in Ohio, which makes me worry that he doesn't *want* to tell me. And then a small, shallow, horrid part of me hopes it's because he's having a miserable time there, and not because he doesn't want to tell me about how, despite the international school, he has met hordes of Chelseas and Madisons and other girls with stupid names who are throwing themselves at him while he basks in their all-American attention and they do the splits in tiny skirts and other over-athletic-y cheerleader things.

I am a terrible person. I should just trust him, and hope he's having a marvellous time, and know he loves only me, and the cheerleaders can high-kick all they want in front of him. But I'm too worried that I can't compare and he will forget me, and so yes, yes, I would rather he was miserable and pining and just doesn't want to keep saying that. This is not something I can tell anyone, not even Jas. Only my dear diary can know what a truly black and wretched soul I have!

Anyway, in other news apart from 'Lila is a bitch', yesterday I went to an open day at Bristol University.

I had thought I was the only one going from our friends, until Ben asked at lunch on Thursday if anyone else was going to Bristol, and it turned out Andy was too, so we all got the train together and had a lovely day. Ben and Andy were both looking at Archaeology – Ben had decided that might be a good idea after Mrs Carruthers had (not so gently) suggested that French might not be Ben's thing. It was *much* more relaxing than the trip to Edinburgh, with Dad nudging me and insisting I should ask questions in the presentations and then, even worse, asking questions himself.

Bristol on my own was far better. I didn't have to ask anything and just got to feel sorry for other poor souls being mortified by their parents, instead of me. And then exploring the city centre afterwards was also much preferable to the awkward walk around Edinburgh where Mum and Dad would start with, 'Oh look, do you remember –' and then break off as Anita looked increasingly bootfaced at all the reminders of their relationship.

I sent Nicky a long email about our day, and everything we did and saw. Ben and Andy made Archaeology sound really interesting, and I wondered if I should go to another open day and look at that – widen my scope from just English? I asked Nicky what he thought, in the hope that it might prompt him to then be a little more forthcoming on his own university plans.

Perhaps, in fact, I should be considering Psychology, with this sort of insight into people? But do I really want to spend my days listening to other people's problems? Some of them might be quite interesting, but of course you're not allowed to tell anyone what you've been told. And I suspect I would want to tell a lot of people just to pull themselves together, which I think is frowned upon in psychologists. It's the same problem with Medicine.

Archaeology would not involve having to put up with people and their secret problems – apart from dead ones, whose problems I could share with anyone. I know it's not all Indiana Jones adventures and mystery-solving and Nazi-thwarting of course, but Archaeology has a lot of scope. I shall consult Andy and Ben further before making any decisions!

EMILY

CHAPTER NINE

A thought has occurred to me.

Reading Mum's other diary, I got embarrassingly far through it before realising that Lila's gorgeous friend Tom was in fact Uncle Tom, the closest thing I have to a godfather. He is the nicest, kindest person you could ever hope to meet. Mum is still friends with other people from her diary too, like Auntie Kate and Auntie Jas, who are also pretty cool and good to have around. I think I could probably go to any of those three if I had a problem that I couldn't talk to Mum or Dad about. Despite her determination to be that sort of person to me, Stella doesn't realise that this is not something you can just make happen. Either you are or you aren't, and she definitely isn't.

Now Lila is talking more and more about someone called Andy – and my dad's name is Andrew. Before I read any further, I need to know if he is the Andy from the diary, because I simply cannot witness my parents' origin story in real time, it would be far, FAR too cringe. What if she goes into *detail* about him? Lila can overshare quite a lot. I don't need to know that sort of stuff about my parents. As far as I'm concerned, they met and I was created through some sort of immaculate conception arrangement when they were in their early thirties, and then they went their separate ways with no physical unpleasantness *whatsoever*.

But if Dad *is* the Andy from the diary, and they get together over the course of this volume – since obviously at some point Lila and Nicky must've split up or Nicky would be my father – then I will be forced to confront the disgusting truth that my parents Have Done It. And not only that – they have possibly Done It *more than once*. I do not need that sort of nastiness in my life. Though I suppose the psychological trauma might distract me from being miserable about Oli and stressing over whether Poppy is ghosting me for Grace.

I heard Dad come home just then, and I ran downstairs to see if my fears were unfounded. Annoyingly, he had Stella with him. I wondered if I should wait until it was just me and Dad to ask him if he was *the* Andy, but that could take days if Stella's previous form is anything to go by. Either she's clinging to Dad like a limpet to show off what a good girlfriend she is, or she's trying to bond with me to show Dad what good wife and mother material she is. Unlike Granny Anita, she doesn't even have Border terriers to mitigate how irritating she is.

'Hi, Dad,' I said, and then somewhat grudgingly, 'Hi, Stella. Dad, can I ask you something?'

'Of course,' Dad said, flicking through his post. 'Stella's offered to cook tonight, by the way.'

'I'm going to make my famous lentil bake,' Stella said in the special warm voice she uses to talk to me, so Dad sees how caring she is, and my heart sank. But at least, once she had bustled off into the kitchen, it gave me a chance to ask Dad my burning question about how he and Mum had met.

Dad frowned. 'Why do you want to know that now, Emily?'

'I just . . . I just wondered. I'm just . . . taking an interest.'

'Well, we met at sixth form college, actually.'

Oh no. Dad *was* the Andy from the diary.

'Right.' I gulped. 'So were you together all the time from sixth form college until I was born? Well, until you split up?'

'No. No, we were just friends at college. It wasn't till university that we –'

We were interrupted by an anguished wail from the kitchen, and we rushed through, thinking Stella must've hurt herself somehow, only to find her just outside the back door, where she had fallen dramatically to her knees, clutching some of the now rather shrivelled weeds I had so helpfully pulled up earlier and had left lying in the sun to die.

Unfortunately it turned out they weren't weeds at all, but were the remains of Stella's precious herb garden, without which, she wept, she could not possibly make her lentil bake. Then there was a bit of an awkward moment when I said I was sorry, of course, but was it really worth crying over some herbs, and Dad snapped at me not to be so cheeky and to apologise to Stella, and told me off for not being more careful – like, how was I to know what parsley even looks like?

Dad then suggested a takeaway for dinner, which suited me just fine, but Stella made a lot of noise about how it wouldn't be nearly as beneficial for our gut health, and Dad said it was Friday night, a treat wouldn't hurt, and promised he would take her to the garden centre in the morning to buy more plants. Stella just sniffed that, actually, she'd have to replant everything again from organic seed, because *who knew* what pesticides and GM FrankenPlants the garden centre might unleash upon us.

Dinner was a bit strained. Stella spent the whole meal picking at her tofu and looking martyred while making pointed remarks about all the lovely things she could have cooked for us if only she had some fresh herbs, and seemed completely unmoved by my explanations. On the plus side, though, she actually went home after dinner, looking extremely long-suffering, and announcing she would be back in the morning with seeds to start again.

Dad looked quite relieved at the lack of the Famous Lentil Bake (more like infamous, if you ask me, given it looks, smells and tastes exactly like sick). He produced some ice cream after our takeaway, which I was starting to realise was his preamble to a 'serious talk'. I hoped this was the time for us to resume our chat about his relationship with Mum. But he wanted to talk to me about 'making more of an effort' and 'at least *trying* to get on with Stella'.

I huffily concurred I would *try*, but I couldn't promise anything. I reminded Dad that the annihilation of the herb garden had been a genuine mistake, and I really had just been trying to help! Dad finally sighed and said that it might be a nice gesture if I offered to help Stella plant her seeds in the morning, and I reluctantly agreed, if only to get back to the subject in hand – namely Mum and Dad.

'Why are you so interested in how your mum and I met?' Dad looked a bit confused.

'Well,' I said awkwardly. 'I take it Mum told you about Oli?'

Obviously, she had. Why else all the hushed phone calls about how *tricky* I was being, and the special voice chats. But I explained how Mum had given me her old diary to read, to help me see that heartbreak is just part of growing up, and how she'd kept mentioning a boy called Andy, and suddenly I had the ick that it might be Dad and I didn't want to read any more if she was going to say stuff about him as anything other than a friend.

Dad looked sort of wistful and hopeful and said, 'I mean, yes, lots of people call me Andy, and I was at college with Lila, but it might not be me she's talking about. Andy's quite a common name.'

'Did you go on an open day at Bristol Uni with her and a boy called Ben?'

Dad looked cross for a moment and then laughed. 'Yes, I did. I only went because Lila said she was going and I thought it might be a chance to spend the day a with her. And then she might notice me as more than a friend. But that boy Ben hung around the whole time too.'

'So there *was* something between you and Lila at college?' I persisted.

Dad sighed and explained that no – no, there hadn't been. He had very much wanted there to be – 'I thought she was perfect, I was mad about her' – but Lila didn't see him like that.

'You were properly friend-zoned!' I interrupted.

Dad supposed 'friend-zoned' was a good description for what had happened to him. And then, he said, they'd ended up both going to Bristol University, and had a brief thing there, which petered out. They'd lost touch after that, but then a few years later, they had stumbled over each other again through the medium of Facebook, and ended up getting married and having me.

'Ugh, old people's socials,' I said in disgust.

'It wasn't old people's socials then!' Dad protested. 'It was new! And cool! Everyone was sending friend requests to everyone they'd ever known. So we got chatting again, and then we met up and we –'

'LALALALALA!' I shouted, fingers in my ears.

Dad reminded me that I was the one who'd asked about Mum and him.

'Only because I didn't want to inadvertently read about something inappropriate taking place between my *parents,*' I hissed.

Dad was a little huffy at that and told me I was being very childish if I couldn't cope with the idea of my parents having a relationship, and then we had a row because I'm SO SICK of people telling me I'm *childish* and *immature*.

'How would YOU like to read all the details of Grandma and Grandpa kissing – or worse?' I shrieked. 'All I wanted was a little heads-up about what to expect from the diary, that's all!'

'WHY DON'T YOU ASK YOUR BLOODY MOTHER THEN!' roared Dad. 'How should I know what's in her damn diary? She's the one who wrote it, she's the one who gave it to you. She hardly knew I even existed in those days, so I think it's a bit unfair of you to expect *me* to know what she's going to say next!'

'I only asked you because you're *here*,' I yelled. 'And so I thought *maybe* you'd make some time to talk to me, like you're always telling me you want to, but actually I think you're just annoyed I'm here, cramping your style with *Stella*, and you don't even want me, and Mum doesn't want me, all she cares about is her stupid novel, and Oli doesn't want me, and Poppy doesn't either. No one wants me. I hate you all. And now you're telling me that I'm the one being unfair to *you*, when NO ONE IS EVER FAIR TO ME!' And with that, I burst into tears and ran upstairs to lock myself in my room.

As I started flinging my clothes and my laptop and make-up and everything else I'd brought with me into my bags, I was quite hurt Dad hadn't even *bothered* to follow me and try and make things up. But why should I be surprised?

No one cared about me.

Mum had been thrilled to see the back of me for the summer. Poppy had immediately gone over to the enemy the minute I was off the scene. And Oli – well. The less said about *him* the better. And all I had to try and make me feel better was some crappy diary my mother had written back in the dark ages when she didn't even have washi tape to stick her stupid emails and letters into the book with, so they were all falling out because she'd used Sellotape which had now dried up and gone yellow and was cracking. And *this* was supposed to comfort me and bring light to my darkness, and succour to my shrivelled and unloved heart?

I sat down and had a little cry for a bit, to give Dad a chance to come upstairs and tell me he was sorry and that he loved me more than Stella, and that everything would be all right. But he didn't come. Instead, I could hear him downstairs, on the phone again to Mum, shouting, 'For crying out loud, Lila, what am I supposed to do with her?'

That finished it for me. He very clearly had no further wish for me to stay with him. I was nothing more than a hindrance. I'd even tried to help by making my fortune as a gardening TikTokker and everyone had just been cross with me because of some stupid plants. Plants grew back eventually! Everyone knew that.

It would serve them all right if I ran away. Maybe I could go and stay with Uncle Tom. But I wouldn't tell anyone where

I was going, not even Tom, until I was there. Let them sweat a bit. Be sorry that Mum had had the nerve to tell Dad I was 'difficult'. That when Stella had dramatically said to Dad in the kitchen (when they thought I couldn't hear) that she felt like I had murdered her children, because her plants were her *babies,* Dad hadn't told her to pull herself together, and that plants were in no way like children, but instead he'd just said, 'I know they're very important to you, darling.' Like he actually thinks I'm a murderer and this is all my fault.

Maybe that's why he's on the phone to Mum right now. He's trying to send me back because he's worried about being under the same roof as a plant-baby murderer. Maybe Mum doesn't want me back either. I'll probably get to Tom's and he'll have already heard about me and will turn me out on to the moors. I'll have to live in a cave.

Would that be so bad? Maybe not, if it was quite a big cave, beside a waterfall? I've always wanted to live beside a waterfall. And I could forage for berries and nuts on the moor. And maybe there would be a wildcat called Bob, but I would tame it, and it would be my friend and companion, and no one would ever know where I had gone, and then they would be sorry.

I could worry about what the wildcat and I would eat and how we would keep warm in the winter when the time came.

I was quite enchanted with my new vision of a simpler life, without all the people who had treated me so unfairly. From now on, it would just be me and Bob the wildcat. I did not need anyone. My solitary life on the moors with Bob would make me very wise, and as I got older, the local folk would worship me like a goddess of the moors, and bring me offerings. That was probably how Bob and I would get through the winters. The people of the villages would bring us cosy blankets and food, for they would now be unable to live without my sage advice.

I wonder if you get 5G in a cave? And if the villagers would bring me a power pack every week?

I picked up my bags and stamped downstairs. I wanted Dad to hear me leaving and later be filled with regret when he realised I wasn't just having a teenage tantrum but was in fact gone for good. Perhaps one day, when he was very old, word would reach me (or maybe I would have a Vision in the waterfall, or the fire in my cave) that he was on his deathbed, and I would leave my cave and my moors, and go to him. He would gasp at how beautiful I had become in my simple life, and beg my forgiveness, which I would magnanimously bestow.

Oooh, I wonder if I could make TikTok videos about natural beauty products I make from the things I find in my foraging, which give me a glowing wild rose complexion, and everyone will be stunned by how clever I am (as well as WISE!)?

I wrenched open the front door (not that easy when you're laden with all your worldly possessions), and Dad appeared in the sitting-room doorway, still on the phone to Mum.

'I'll need to call you back, Lila,' he said, and hung up. 'Emily, what do you think you're doing?'

'I'm leaving,' I said coldly. 'Because no one wants me and no one l-l-l-loves me, so I'm just g-g-going and I hope you'll all b-b-be very happy without m-m-m-meeeee!' And I burst into tears.

I hadn't meant to cry. I'd intended to be very aloof and dignified and make it clear that I didn't even *care*. But I couldn't help it. Because I *did* care, of course I did, and I didn't really want to go and live in a cave, even if it did finally make me into a famous TikTokker, and how do you even go to the toilet in a cave? And so the tears suddenly came unbidden, and instead of striding off into my new life, collecting Bob the wildcat on the way, I just stood in Dad's hall, sobbing pitifully.

'Oh, Emily.' Dad looked stricken. 'How can you think that?'

I gulped something incoherent that was meant to be, 'Because you *don't* love me, and you don't want me and I didn't mean to kill the stupid plants,' but I was crying too much and I don't think he understood. But it didn't matter, because he gave me an enormous hug and we stood there for a while, with me crying so hard I did wonder if I might rupture something, and Dad just stroking my hair and rocking me gently and telling me that I was his daughter and he loved me more than anything in the world and everything was going to be all right.

After a while, I managed to take a deep breath and attempted to wipe my nose and my eyes. Dad's shirt had been rather a casualty of the storm, and was drenched in my tears and liberally streaked with snot.

'Doesn't matter,' Dad said. 'It'll wash. Why don't you come and sit down and tell me all about it?'

So I left my bags in the hall and went into the sitting room with Dad and tried to explain about everything. Not just about Oli ('Lost cause,' Dad insisted. 'Stupid boy. His loss.') and Poppy ('Darling, if you're that upset, just swallow your pride and ring her and say sorry!'), and then when I made incredulous noises at the thought of *ringing* Poppy and *talking* to her, or indeed talking to *anyone* on the phone, especially anyone of my age: 'Well, text her then, or SnapChat her, or whatever it is you do to communicate. The point is, you can still fix this, but the longer it goes on, the harder it will be to fix, so just tell her you're sorry and you miss her, and you'll probably find she feels the same way.'

Most of all, though, I finally told Dad my biggest secret. Something I have been increasingly worried about for the last few years. That I felt like I was responsible for his and Mum's marriage ending.

I was only four when they split up. They said all the right things at the time – they both still loved me more than anything, they just didn't love each other *like that* any more, it was nothing to do with me, they didn't want to live together any more for grown-up reasons, etc. But as I got older, a nagging doubt had grown into a conviction that *I* was to blame. My very existence had ruined their relationship. The strain of looking after me had driven them apart, and they would both have been happier without me. And that they resented me for it and wished I had never been born.

Dad was aghast.

'Emily . . .' He grasped for words. '*Nothing* could be further from the truth. It really was nothing to do with you, and everything to do with Lila and me. Neither of us resent you, and neither of us could even begin to *imagine* life without you, let alone *wish* for a life without you. Emily, sweetheart, you are my reason for getting up in the morning. The joy in my life. Even when everything seems bleak and grey, there is always a light for me when I think of you.'

'Even when Stella makes you eat lentil bake?' I hiccupped, trying to make a tiny joke.

'Especially when Stella makes me eat lentil bake,' Dad told me solemnly. 'I choke it down, reminding myself how good it is for me, much better than chips, delicious though they are, and how much the lentil bake increases my chances of spending many more years with my beautiful daughter and seeing her grow up and become even more amazing than she already is. Goodness, sometimes that's the only way I can get it down. That and ketchup,' he added.

'Really?'

'Really,' Dad promised. 'And I'm sorry if I've been busy, or grumpy, or made you feel I don't have time for you, or that I'm putting Stella ahead of you. You are the most important thing in my life, and I will make more effort to make sure you know that in future.'

'OK.' I was starting to feel better, and I was very glad to be able to abandon my cave plan. 'But why *did* you and Mum split up then? When you'd known each other for so long?'

'There were a lot of reasons,' Dad said slowly. 'But the main ones were, I think, Lila never entirely unfriend-zoned me, she wanted true love and she resented me for not being the love of her life. And I hadn't realised that even when you end up with the love of *your* life, the perfect dream girl you've longed for forever, no one can live up to that ideal. The bins still need putting out, someone has to go to Sainsbury's, the freezer needs defrosting. And so, in the end, I resented her too, because I thought it would just be a happily ever after. But I can never regret marrying Lila, because I got you. Do you understand?'

I sniffed. 'I think so. Who was the love of Mum's life then? Was it Nicky?'

Dad looked rather sad as he rubbed his eyes and said yes, it may well have been Nicky, because in all the time he'd known her, he'd never seen her look at anyone else in the way she'd looked at Nicky. And that she'd never been quite the same after things ended between them. But he didn't know what had happened, or why it had ended.

I suddenly felt a wave of exhaustion sweep over me. All the crying and emotion and potential running away to a cave with a wildcat called Bob had been very draining. Now I had a great longing to be tucked up in bed, even though I was really enjoying Dad talking to me like an equal for once. And though I couldn't say this to Dad, of course, I suddenly wanted to keep reading Lila's diary and find out what happened with Nicky that had changed her so much and left her eternally searching for the perfect love.

Dad had also given me a lot to think about when he mentioned building Lila up into an impossible, perfect dream girl. Was that what I'd done with Oli? Maybe I hadn't been in love with Oli *himself* so much as the *idea* of the slightly older, cooler boy being so interested in me. And maybe it hadn't been love and my broken heart *was* just hurt pride, especially given the very public way he'd chosen to dump me!

For the first time, I felt a shred of anger amidst the pain. Really, if you looked at it objectively, Oli was not a good person. In fact, it occurred to me that it was possible he was not some flawless, unattainable creature that I had been lucky to be noticed by, but a selfish idiot who didn't deserve me wasting my summer pining for him. If Grace Walker was stupid enough to go out with him after knowing how he'd behaved to me, well, that was her problem. Maybe I wasn't over Oli yet, but at that moment *my* problem was making things up with Poppy. Which was another reason to go upstairs to bed – so I could message her and try to apologise.

Dad gave me a hand back up the stairs with all my stuff and then we said goodnight. As I went to the bathroom to brush my teeth, I heard him on the phone again, saying, 'Lila? Hi. She's OK, I think. We've had a good chat. I'd forgotten how *hard* it is being a teenager. How it feels like everyone is against you. But yeah, I think we've sorted some things out, and hopefully she's feeling better . . .'

Once I was in bed, I messaged Poppy. I wrote and deleted and wrote and deleted it about a dozen times, trying to find exactly the right words to explain and hopefully make Poppy both see my point of view, and forgive me. Eventually, I settled on –

> I'm so so sorry I don't h8 u U r my best m8 I was just v upset about stupid Oli Grace is welcome to him I just want us to be friends again Pls 4give me I was so stupid to say all that stuff I didn't mean it M8s? Pls? xxxx

But I still couldn't send it. What if she didn't reply? What if she'd blocked my number? There were so many 'what ifs'. As long as I hadn't sent the message, I could still persuade myself that everything was all right and Poppy and I could make up. If I sent it, though, and Poppy didn't reply – or worse, didn't even read it – then I'd have to get a lot more creative with the 'what ifs'. Like, what if she's not replying because she's at the cinema, watching a really long film? Or . . . what if something awful has happened to her?

Now I started worrying that I might have *caused* something awful to happen to Poppy by imagining it and so making it happen! What if she was lying in hospital even now, gravely ill? She could have been in a car accident! She could have eaten something poisonous, like a deadly mushroom! Except Poppy doesn't eat mushrooms, she hates them. Maybe she *accidentally* ate a mushroom? Anyway, she could be dying and I wouldn't even know! What if I went home to check on her?

I reminded myself it was now eleven o'clock at night, and there was no way Dad was going to make a two-hour drive to take me back to Mum's on the off-chance Poppy was on her death bed. Then inspiration struck! I could check where she was on our Life 360 circle! Why hadn't I thought of that before?

I quickly opened the app. Poppy wasn't there. Was she already dead and her parents had deleted it? Or, the more rational part of my mind suggested, had Poppy removed herself from our circle?

This was *so much* worse than I'd anticipated.

Poppy must be *really* angry with me. Or dead. No, not dead. Just angry.

I tried to find a glimmer of hope. What if she'd had a row with her parents too, and gone to be a wise woman in a cave? But even then, if she was living in a cave with no signal, I'd still be able to see the last place she HAD had signal – and she was just gone.

I tried to be positive and not despair. Maybe there'd been a massive thunderstorm at home that had knocked out all the mobile masts. Did Life 360 use phone masts, or GPS? What if a meteor had hit the satellite that was tracking Poppy on Life 360? That sounded entirely possible. Meteors were always hitting things and causing destruction. Look at the dinosaurs. If a meteor could wipe out the dinosaurs, it could *definitely* break a satellite.

That must be exactly what had happened. Satellites probably take a long time to fix, being up in space and all that. They'd have to send a rocket and it's not like people just have rockets lying around, apart from Elon Musk. So the satellite people will have to persuade Elon Musk to lend them a spare rocket and then get it into space and *then* fix the satellite. That could take days. Weeks even.

In the meantime, while Elon Musk's altruism was being appealed to, I would distract myself with Lila's diary for a bit, and then I would go to sleep. And who knows? Maybe Elon Musk will be feeling kind and generous and be like, oh hey, yeah, take a rocket, no probs, I've got loads of them, and by the morning the satellite could be fixed!

LILA

CHAPTER TEN

SATURDAY 1ST NOVEMBER 1997

Tonight is Kate's dad's big fireworks party. Like everything at the moment, I *wanted* to look forward to it and be excited, but it reminded me so much of Nicky - all I could think about was how badly I'd behaved to Nicky at the party last year. He'd been so clever, setting up a system to remotely set off the fireworks in time to music, and delighting Kevin who usually had to pay a company vast sums of money to do that.

And then, after the fireworks, Nicky had told me how he felt about me. On a cold bench in Kate's garden, my head still full of stars and rockets, my ears ringing with the explosions and the music, with the sounds of laughter and chatter from the bonfire and the smell of woodsmoke and cordite lingering in the air, Nicky had taken my hand and told me that he loved me. That he'd always loved me. And I . . . I had said I didn't feel the same way. I had said

I couldn't go out with him, because what would people think? That is possibly one of the worst things I have ever said and done.

If I could sit on that bench again, with the same crisp autumn air around us, and the same starbursts of colour and noise fading in the distance, and Nicky could kiss me and tell me he loved me again, except this time I would kiss him back and tell him how much I loved him too – well, that would go a long way to reducing the shame I felt about that night.

I so wanted to tell him this. But his last email was so abrupt that I didn't like to. The emails seem to be all I get now. There have only ever been two letters, and I have given up telling myself that any more have been lost in the post. Even if they had, given we had promised to write every day, surely *some* letters would have arrived?

I tried to comfort myself about the lack of letters at first by telling myself that Nicky probably didn't realise how much more I loved receiving actual paper letters instead of just emails. I firmly told myself that it was *what* he wrote, not *how* he wrote it that was important. But even the emails are getting shorter and shorter (quite a feat, given that they weren't exactly long in the first place), and I'm struggling not to give in to despair that Nicky has found someone else in Ohio.

I don't want to be all desperate and needy, demanding to know what's going on and making a fool of myself if I'm reading too much into things, but something is definitely not right. Maybe it's just Nicky being a boy, and far more into science than reading and romance like me? But then I remember last year, and the messages we would exchange on the college chatroom, before we knew who we were talking to. Such long, funny, clever messages Nicky would send, so unlike his brief, brusque emails now.

I tried talking to Jas about it, and whether I should ask Nicky outright what was going on. Jas thought not. She gave me some hope, pointing out what a huge upheaval it must have been for Nicky, moving to Ohio so suddenly like that, trying to make friends and settle in to a completely alien environment. And it's not even like Nicky has watched all the films and programmes about American high schools that we have! He's never even seen *Heathers*! And he's quite sniffy about *Beverley Hills 90210*. So he'll have had *no* idea what to expect; it will have been a total culture shock for him.

Jas was right, of course, though I wasn't sure I found her words as comforting as she'd meant them to be.

I asked her if she thought it really was like in the TV programmes, though, and she said maybe it wasn't so much like *Heathers*, because even in America it's probably frowned upon to go around murdering your classmates because they're annoying (if only it wasn't, though, just *who* would I possibly think about murdering . . .).

But I did worry the rest of it might be like the films, even at the international school, with everyone glamorous and mature, and with amazing clothes instead of my Topshop jeans, and instead of getting the bus, they can all drive and have their own cars. My own attempt at driving ended in ignominy as my driving instructor returned me home after my third lesson, refunded the rest of the course and said Mum was lucky he wasn't claiming damages from her for the stress of trying to teach me to drive. This seemed unreasonable, just because I had tried to go to round a roundabout the wrong way, which frankly could happen to anyone. Mum tutted and said clearly the instructor was feeble and *she* would teach me to drive. After one lesson with her, where I only *nearly* ran over a toddler, Mum declared public transport was better for the environment anyway and has refused to take me out again. Jas tried to cheer me up by reminding me that Cher couldn't drive in *Clueless,* in fact her inability to drive was a major plot point, so surely they couldn't *all* drive.

Cher is the only one in an American high school film who can't drive, though, so non-drivers must be in the minority, and anyway, if Nicky had the choice between me who can't drive, or Alicia Silverstone who can't drive, who would he pick? I know who I would, given that choice.

Jas, with the brutality only a best friend can demonstrate, said yes, but I was shallow, and Nicky wasn't like that, and didn't care about things like clothes or money or glamour, or he'd be in love with Kate, like most of the other boys are. Or he'd fancy Rachel, though she's far too obvious with it, and I don't think her dad is as rich as she likes to make out. (Also, no one's actually in love with her, because she's a terrible person, they just fancy her. At least the boys who are in love with Kate are mostly in love with her because she's so nice, and not because of how rich Kevin is.) 'But, Nicky,' Jas pointed out. 'Nicky is only and has only ever been in love with *you*.'

None of this explained the increasingly terse missives from him, though. Could you even call a three-sentence email a 'missive'? A 'missive' implies an important document, concerning either passionate affairs of the heart, or grand affairs of state. Missives bear wax seals and are handed over by mysterious gentlemen in green velvet cloaks, or comely, blushing maidservants, entrusted with the secrets of their mistresses' hearts. *Missives* do not consist of such poetically heartstopping lines such as:

They don't have Guy Fawkes Night in America. And I think you'll find that the point of Guy Fawkes Night isn't to celebrate someone trying to blow up Parliament, but rather the opposite, it's in celebration of the Gunpowder Plot being stopped and the conspirators being executed. I'm sure you'll still manage to enjoy the party, though.

Well, how was I supposed to know? It made sense to me that we light bonfires and set off fireworks in honour of an anarchic attempt to bring down the government of the day, rather than commemorating Guy Fawkes being burned at the stake. It does make Fireworks Night seem a bit less fun, when you realise that. And Nicky's last line there was distinctly snippy.

I have decided, under the circumstances of Nicky's uncommunicativeness, to avoid seeming sad and pathetic and clingy, so I'm simply replying with friendly jolliness. Now when I write, I will no longer be making any mention of love, or our relationship, or what he means to me, or how bleak it is without him. My emails (I am not going to send any more letters, clearly he can't be bothered sending them to me, so I doubt he wants to receive them either) will be a *masterclass* in Nothing More Than Friendly. And so, should there have been a very important letter gone missing somewhere mid-Atlantic, in which Nicky no doubt is terribly kind but basically says, 'You're chucked,' I won't appear to have been a pathetic loser continuing to bombard him with my undying love, but will be perceived as nothing more than an informative, and slightly brisk, pen pal.

I know deep down this is a feeble approach. We are both being feeble, really. No doubt due to some notion of Noble Honour, Nicky probably feels it would not be good form to dump me by email or letter when he is out there living it up in Ohio, with a cheerleader doing the splits for him, and so will probably feel he has to wait to see me face to face to tell me it's over. Which is really quite bad form, if he is over there snogging Perky All-American Blondes who can drive.

And me . . . well, I know I should push the issue and ask exactly what is going on – maybe even be terribly understanding and say it's fine if he wants to end things, perhaps even intimate that it would probably be the sensible thing to do for both of us. But I'm too afraid that he will immediately reply in huge relief and say yes, yes, he totally agrees, he just hadn't known how to tell me.

Or worse, that he'll be incredulous and tell me there's nothing to end, we're just friends after all, surely I hadn't thought he would want to keep going out with me when he was so far away and he'd assumed I would feel the same and hadn't I even realised that it was over?

This is my very darkest scenario. That not only does Nicky not love me any more, but that I will make a complete fool of myself about it.

And so I will send jolly, *jolly* emails about who said what at lunch and who sat next to who, and what Rachel has done now, and what Mrs Carruthers' latest withering put-down to Ben was in French class, and what happened at the parties and who was there, and all the things you might tell a *friend* who had gone away for a bit. While hoping all the time that Nicky and I are still so much more than friends.

I longed and longed to tell Nicky how much I wished he was going to be at the party tonight, and how I wanted to make it up to him for being so dreadful last year, and how the thing I wanted most in the world was to stand with his arms around me, watching the fireworks, shivering slightly in the chill of the night, but feeling the warmth of him holding me, until the fireworks finished and he kissed me on and on and on under the stars.

Instead (jolly jolly jolly, remember!), I told him how cross Kevin is that he has had to get the fireworks company to do the display, since Nicky isn't here, and that Ben was picking me up (Ben has passed his driving test, he would fit right in in an American high school film now), and what I was going to wear, and how Jas was supposed to be coming over to get ready, but then Dan Wilcox had asked her if she wanted to go to the party with him, and she *actually said yes*, which suggests she's getting over her Man-Hating Phase, but means it's just me that Ben is picking up, because when I asked Tom if he wanted Ben to give him a lift, he was very cagey and said he had something to do first and would see us there.

I wonder if Tom has found a date, like Jas seems to have?

Dan Wilcox is obviously a bit of a spanner in the works for the whole Jas 'n' Ben matchmaking plan. And obviously I couldn't tell Nicky about that, because he would disapprove of meddling in people's lives. I did tell Nicky how embarrassing Mum was about Ben picking me up, though, insisting he come inside and meet her so she could assess if he was responsible enough to drive her daughter around, or if he was some mad boy racer. I wasn't too worried, though, I feel like Ben is the sort of boy that parents just like, so Mum was sure to say he was fine to give me a lift to the party and back.

Then, because I wanted to make myself seem super popular and busy, I finished by saying I needed to go and get ready for the party, because Ben would be here soon – but of course, I had loads of time, which is why I've spent the last hour catching up with my diary. But now it's occurred to me that the 'need to get ready' line for Nicky might seem a bit odd. The trouble with emails as opposed to letters is that you can see what time they were sent, and he might wonder why I was getting ready for a party at 3 p.m., when it doesn't start till 7 p.m.

Actually, I'm overthinking things. I doubt Nicky will even notice the time or be that invested in my life to care if he does. But I'm going to wear my new top, and my favourite boots and my best coat to the party, and pretend I'm wearing them for him, so I look nice when I imagine him kissing me. I described what I was wearing to him so he'll know what I look like, on the off chance he imagines being at the party too, and kissing me under the stars. The stars will probably definitely have to be imagined, though. I think it's going to rain.

I'm home from the party now, but I can't sleep, because I think tonight was what football people describe as a game of two halves.

It started wonderfully. The fireworks were spectacular, even better than the display Nicky put together for Kevin last year, though naturally I wouldn't tell him that. Nicky had gone for the obvious musical choice of Tchaikovsky and the '1812 Overture', but this year the music was something shimmering and strange and wonderful and exactly like fireworks in musical form, if music could be fireworks. It sent shivers down my spine, and I asked Kevin what it was, and he said he hadn't a clue, and called over one of the fireworks men to ask, who said it was Debussy's 'Feux d'Artifice'. Which I suppose makes sense, that a piece of music called 'Fireworks' is so exactly like fireworks.

Kevin had also hired a band for *after* the fireworks as a surprise. I was very glad I'd dressed up and wasn't wearing my scruffy old jeans and trainers! The band was on the big terrace outside, and it was cold, but we were all so busy dancing that it kept us warm. I think I danced with everyone, Tom and Andy and Ben and Luke, and so many other people, including Kevin, who is the nicest man in the world. I thanked him for such a splendid party, and he laughed and said he'd invited some of his clients along too, so the whole thing was tax deductible. I'm not sure what that means, but Kevin seemed pleased about it. I thought it sounded like something I could casually mention in an email to Nicky, without admitting I didn't know what it was, and then I would appear clever and knowledgeable about tax and money and other grown-up matters.

Sometimes I feel like I spend my whole life nodding and smiling and pretending to know what people are talking about.

In a break from dancing, I sat on the steps of the terrace with Tom, and asked what he'd been up to before the party, and he looked secretive and made vague noises about just having stuff to do, but then he started grinning and said, 'Oh, I don't know why I don't just tell you! I *think* I had a date!'

I was thrilled and gave him a huge hug and demanded ALL the details, of course, because a date is a big enough deal as it is, but it's an even bigger deal for Tom, because of stupid people who are not accepting of who he is.

Tom, it seems, has been spending a lot of Saturdays in a new coffee shop in town. In fact, I had gone there with him a couple of weeks ago. Tom admitted he had taken me along as sort of bait because there was this cute boy there that he really liked but wasn't sure if Tom was 'his type'.

'What happened to your one hundred per cent accurate, never fails you gaydar?' I asked indignantly.

'I might have exaggerated a *bit* about it *never* failing,' Tom grumbled. He was, like *ninety-five per cent* sure the boy was into him, but he just wanted to make sure.

I had *thought* Tom was behaving quite oddly that day. And then when we left the coffee shop, instead of walking home with me or suggesting we went to look in HMV or the second-hand bookshop we both loved, he immediately announced he'd forgotten something and needed to go back, and when I said I would wait, practically *shooed* me away.

It turned out he had dashed back into the coffee shop to retrieve his hat which he had accidentally-on-purpose forgotten, and then had managed to strike up a conversation again with the boy in the coffee shop, who had indeed taken Tom's unsubtle 'bait' in the form of me, and enquired if I was Tom's girlfriend. At which point Tom decided he had nothing to lose except a spiralling caffeine habit, and said no, just a friend, and then added that girls weren't really his thing. At which point, Jon, as it turned out Coffee Boy was called, had brightened up immeasurably and suggested they go for a coffee together somewhere else.

'I'd had two cappuccinos with you already, but I wanted to look mature and sophisticated so I had a double espresso with Jon, and then I didn't know if I was shaking with love or caffeine,' sighed Tom, misty-eyed.

Jon lives in the next town but has a Saturday job here because his aunt owns the coffee shop. And he can drive and has his own car. He asked Tom if he wanted to go for a drive after work. And then Tom just smirked and said cars are very useful if you want a little privacy and somewhere to be alone . . . though he insisted nothing much had happened, because it was a Mini and Tom's six foot two. 'But we had a very nice time. And that's all I'm saying!'

I was so thrilled for Tom. I asked why he hadn't brought Jon along to the party. I knew neither Kate nor Kevin would have minded at all; in fact, they would be just as thrilled for him as I was. But Tom said he wanted to keep Jon to himself, because 'right now, it's just me and him and we're both perfect as far as the other is concerned. Do you understand?'.

Tom's eyes were shining brighter than any firework and I assured him that I did understand. I was quite jealous, actually. Nicky and I had known each other for so long, we'd never had that perfect early-stage thing. If anything, we'd always been *too* aware of our faults and imperfections. Maybe that was why he was barely communicating with me now. Perhaps at a distance, he'd had time to reflect and ponder on my many failings and realise that they outweighed my good points.

Tom pulled me to my feet, and we went and danced again before we froze to death. Jas was in the shadows getting extremely friendly with Dan Wilcox. Andy was dancing, rather reluctantly, with Rachel. Kate was dancing *very* closely with a dark-haired boy I didn't recognise. The song was just finishing, and Andy escaped from Rachel with a look of relief as the band announced they were taking a short break. Then Kate rushed over to us, the dark boy in tow, introduced him as Matthew, ordered Tom to get him a drink, and dragged me indoors, where she collapsed dramatically on the stairs and announced she was IN LOVE. 'Oh. My. God! Lila, did you *see* him? Should I kiss him? I've never felt like this!'

Jas and I had been falling in love with random strangers we saw in the street for years, but Kate had always been rather aloof from such romantic endeavours. And now, along came Matthew who seemed to have unleashed the proverbial thunderbolt and Kate was as smitten a kitten as I ever did see.

Kate rushed me up to her room where she feverishly rifled through her drawers to find a Wonderbra and hurled the contents of her (considerable) wardrobe on her bed in search of her shortest skirt.

I was stern, telling her she was being too obvious. If she went back out there with her boobs hoisted to her chin and her skirt up to her breakfast, she would lose all her mystique and allure.

'I could say you spilled a drink on me!' Kate gasped, dragging her sweater off. 'I need to look sexier!'

'NO!' I was more than stern now. 'You are the most gorgeous girl here. You are the most gorgeous girl anywhere you go! If he doesn't fancy you like you are, he isn't going to fancy you because you put on a Wonderbra and a short skirt! Also, feminism!'

Kate was mutinous, despite how she always said it wasn't feminist to dress for men's attention.

'Just go back down there and be yourself,' I ordered. 'Like you always say to me!'

Kate slumped against her bed, somehow still looking elegant and beautiful on the floor in her bra, and whimpered that around Matthew she had no idea how to be herself, and he was at *university* and no doubt surrounded by cultured and mature beauties all day and all night and how could she possibly compete?

I instructed her that this wasn't *Gladiators*, and said we'd better go back out there before Rachel spotted him and tried to muscle in. Back on the terrace, the speed with which Matthew dashed back to Kate's side suggested her fears were unfounded. The band started playing and he swept her off to dance again.

Looked like it was everyone's lucky night. Everyone apart from me.

Suddenly feeling sad, I stumbled down the steps into the garden, dark and quiet now after the fireworks, and set off along the path to the bench where I'd been sitting last year when Nicky found me. I would just sit there for a few minutes and pretend he was with me, holding me close, keeping me warm, brushing the hair out of my eyes and telling me how beautiful I was, and how much he loved me. If everyone else had found someone tonight, surely I could at least pretend?

Maybe I'd get home to find that my email had reminded Nicky of this time last year, and he'd finally found the words to tell me how he feels again, and I would be as buoyed up with love as Tom and Kate. More so, because Nicky and I really know each other, and so I know it *is* love, not infatuation as it undoubtedly is for Kate and Tom at this stage, when they barely know Jon and Matthew. Not that infatuation can't feel very nice. But it's not a patch on what Nicky and I have. Or at least what we did have.

On 'our' bench, I tipped my head back and looked at the stars and tried to think romantic thoughts about how Nicky might be looking at the same stars at that very moment, and so in some ways we were still together even though we were apart. Was there any way I could write that to him without sounding ridiculous?

I don't even know if they are the same stars in Ohio. I have always been slightly confused about the stars changing depending on what hemisphere you're in. Also, there's the time difference, so it probably wasn't even dark in Ohio yet. Maybe I could just say something to him about looking at the stars and asking what the stars are like in Ohio, so he knew I was thinking about him? Did he ever think about me under the Ohio stars? Perhaps there is too much light pollution, given the most romantic thing he has written to me is still his first letter about becoming a mutant rat king trapped under a mall, writing me poems. This now seems achingly lovely, instead of a bit weird as I thought at the time.

So that, believe it or not, was the *good* part of the night. I mean, it *was* good. The fireworks were amazing, and the dancing was fun, and I was so happy for Tom and Kate and Jas that they all seemed to have found someone. It just would have been *better* if Nicky was there.

And of course, if Nicky had been there, the next bit wouldn't have happened.

I was wondering if I could send telepathic messages to Nicky through the stars, and attempt to write a poem to this effect, so at least I had something to show for sitting dramatically alone in the dark while all my friends got off with the love of their lives, when Ben walked down the path towards me.

He held out a blanket and said he'd seen me coming down here and had worried I might be cold. He really did have the most lovely Welsh accent. Then he looked a bit awkward and explained the blanket was from his car, he hadn't stolen it from Kevin's house. His mother made him keep it in the car in case of emergencies. 'I'm not sure what blanket-based emergency she is envisaging, but she insists.

Along with a first-aid kit. She had hoped I might become a doctor, and I think she still harbours notions of me saving lives at a road accident, armed with nothing more than a tartan travel rug, some antiseptic wipes and a packet of plasters!'

I laughed and told him I felt his pain because my parents both wanted me to be a doctor too, and are still getting over the disappointment of realising there is probably no one in the world less suited for Medicine than me!

Ben laughed and said he was possibly equally unsuited because he had cut his finger trying to slice some cheese last year and fainted on the spot, but his mum still hoped that was just a minor impediment to his glittering career healing the sick.

I said my main impediment was the sick themselves, especially vomiting ones. And the whole dealing with people thing. And my desire to just tell them to pull themselves together, which is frowned upon in doctors. And also the minor detail of not being clever enough, but mostly my general irritation with the unwell. Ben chuckled again and then asked if I minded if he sat down.

I shook my head. Ben settled down on the bench beside me and tucked the blanket over us both. He rummaged in his coat pocket and produced a can of beer for me and a Coke for him. Then he flourished a large bag of crisps at me – Kettle Chips, no less. There was no expense spared at Kevin's parties. Mum considered buying Walkers instead of supermarket own brand the height of decadence.

'You're so funny,' said Ben when I told him this. Ben has a strange sense of humour. And then we started talking about what we *do* want to do, since neither of us are suitable for Medicine. I knew of course from the open day in Bristol that he was interested in Archaeology, but we talked for a while about how the course seemed interesting, but was that really what he wanted to do for the rest of his life?

'It's so hard, isn't it?' I sighed, and told him how when I was seven, all I wanted in the world was to be called Belinda. And when I was nine, all I wanted was a Barbie doll, but my mum wouldn't let me have one because she said Barbie was too slutty and American, and Sindy dolls were much more British and wholesome, and when I was fourteen I was utterly convinced that if only I had my ears pierced everything would be all right with my life, and *then* I thought if only I could go to sixth form college and meet – I stopped hastily, because I didn't want Ben to think I was a complete saddo who had only wanted to go to college to meet boys, so I feebly finished with 'new friends' and then rallied and said how ridiculous it is that we're supposed to know who and what we are going to be when we're only seventeen.

Ben said he quite agreed and perhaps he would turn

out to be a polar explorer (I wondered if there were any polar places left to explore, but I didn't like to say that) or managing a paper-clip factory and what point would there have been in an Archaeology degree then?

I said I supposed there was an argument to be made for learning for learning's sake, and also, of course, university sounded quite fun, and then he asked me why I thought I wanted to do English.

I shrugged and said people who studied English usually secretly want to be a writer of some sort. Unless you're Tom; he's not secret about wanting that at all. 'But hardly anyone actually makes a living at it, do they?' I finished. 'So I don't know.'

'You and Tom,' Ben said. 'You seem quite close. Is there anything between you?'

I burst out laughing again, and then remembered Ben didn't know why this should be funny, and it certainly wasn't my place to tell him, so I stifled my laughter and said no, we were just really good friends, that's all.

Ben grinned and said, 'Oh, I'm so glad to hear that. I didn't want to, you know, step on anyone's toes, but I've been wanting to do this since the first day Mrs Carruthers sat me with you in French and I burbled on incessantly about my love of books about trains!'

And before I knew what was happening, Ben leaned

over to me and tucked one big warm hand behind my neck and brushed my fringe out my eyes with his other hand and kissed me.

Now this is where it gets really bad.

It was lovely. And it was such a shock and felt so nice that I found myself kissing him back. He slid his arms around me, moving his hand from my neck down to my waist, *just* like Rachel described it in *Friends* when Ross kissed her for the first time, and I don't even know how it happened, but I had my arms around his neck, and it was far longer than it should have been before I realised that what I was doing was VERY, VERY BAD and I broke off the kiss and shot off to the other end of the bench.

'What are you *doing?*' I gasped.

Ben stammered apologies, and that he hadn't meant to upset me, he really liked me and 'you gave me that look before you went down the steps that I thought meant you wanted me to follow you, and I'm sorry, I'm really sorry!'

I had no idea what look he was talking about; I didn't even remember seeing him on the terrace. I spluttered, 'I have a *boyfriend*!'

'But you said you and Tom . . .?'

'Not Tom.'

'But he's the only guy I ever see you with, like close enough to that he could be a boyfriend. I don't understand, you've never mentioned a boyfriend and –'

Hadn't I ever mentioned Nicky to Ben? I was sure I had. Hadn't I? Maybe I hadn't. Maybe, on some level, I hadn't wanted him to know about Nicky. Was it possible that subconsciously I knew Ben quite fancied me, or at least liked hanging out with me, and I didn't want to stop him feeling like that by reminding him about my long-distance boyfriend in BLOODY OHIO?

'He . . . he's not here right now,' I muttered. 'He's in Ohio.'

Ben looked even more confused and said he'd heard us talking about that guy who moved to Ohio, but how I could be going out with him when he was all the way over there, in *Ohio*?

'He's coming back,' I insisted. 'I . . . it's complicated.'

Ben looked grim but also very handsome while looking grim, as he muttered that he wished I'd mentioned the complicated boyfriend in Ohio thing *before* he had fallen for me, and let him kiss me, and what did this boyfriend in Ohio have that Ben didn't, given he wasn't even on the same *continent*.

'Because you did kiss me back,' he said. 'And you seemed to enjoy it.'

'Yes,' I whispered miserably. How could I possibly explain Nicky to Ben? Nicky wasn't the sort of person you could explain, he just *was*. But at the same time a small, mean part of me thought Ben was right. He was here. Nicky wasn't. And part of the reason I had kissed Ben back was that it was so *nice* to be kissed again. It felt like a very long time since Nicky had gone away and anyone had kissed me. And maybe, if Nicky had had more to say for himself than just a lecture on the true origins of Guy Fawkes Night, I might *not* have been so receptive to kissing Ben – if, say, I'd been sitting here thinking about how nice it was that Nicky was over there in Ohio definitely thinking about *me,* I almost certainly would not have kissed Ben back. Instead, I was at something of a low ebb, both missing Nicky and not being sure if he even remembered who I was, and no one can be blamed for what they do at a low ebb, can they? That's hardly fair.

Also, at this point, it's pure speculation on my part that Nicky is even still my boyfriend. I'm only assuming he is because, so far, he hasn't actually told me he isn't, but for all I know, it's over, and I haven't done anything wrong by kissing Ben, because in fact I am a perfectly free agent, at liberty to kiss whoever I please.

'It's complicated,' was all I could offer again to Ben, who was looking increasingly angry. And handsome. Anger suited him. 'I'm sorry. Ben. I should've told you before. It's just . . . I *think* he's my boyfriend, but I'm not sure.'

Ben got really cross at that and said either I had a boyfriend in Ohio or I didn't, and by the way, if I didn't want him to kiss me again, I didn't have to invent a mysterious mid-western boyfriend, I just had to say I didn't want him to kiss me again.

'But I do want you to kiss me again,' I blurted out before I could stop myself, at which point Ben did not hesitate and kissed me again extremely thoroughly. Afterwards, he said, 'So what was all that about the boyfriend?' and I attempted to explain, but properly this time, saying how confused I was about what was going on between Nicky and me, and also that I was very sorry, but I really shouldn't have kissed him either time, or at least not until I knew for sure that things were over with Nicky.

And then it all went even more wrong as Ben demanded to know what happened if it *wasn't* over with Nicky and I whimpered that then I couldn't kiss him again because Nicky was special, I couldn't exactly explain how, he just was, and then Ben snarled that what I was saying was that if it's over with Nicky, he would do as second best, and then he got up and stormed back to the party, as I cried that I hadn't meant that at all, I was just very *confused.*

I sat there for a moment wondering how this had happened, why *life* had to be so complicated, as well as

Nicky and me. I realised the band had stopped playing and it was getting late and the party was winding down, and I had better go back and see if Tom or someone would walk me home, as I didn't think there was much chance of Ben driving me home now, like we had arranged.

To my astonishment, Ben was standing on the terrace, still looking livid and jangling his car keys, waiting to drive me home because, as he informed me in curt tones (it is really unfair how being angry makes Ben even more attractive), even though I had spurned his advances, he was not the sort of person who would just leave a girl alone to make her own way home. And he turned and stalked off to his car.

Oh God, I thought. Thank goodness I didn't live far away, because this was going to be an extremely awkward journey. But on the other hand, it was very cold and quite far to walk, and if I did have to go and find Tom or Andy and ask them to walk me home, then I'd have to come up with some explanation of why Ben wasn't driving me home as arranged. And until things were resolved one way or the other with Nicky, then the fewer people who knew what had happened between us in the garden, the better! And also, I couldn't deny that given everything I'd just said to Ben, and given the callous way I'd kissed him back, knowing full well that I shouldn't, it really was very chivalrous of him to still be prepared to drive me home, and it would be most ungracious of me not to accept his kind gesture.

Ben didn't talk on the way home. When we got to my house, I decided the best thing to do would be simply to act as if nothing had happened and a helpful friend had just given me a lift after a charming party.

'Goodnight then!' I said brightly, scrambling to open the door and hop out. 'Thank you so much for the lift, much obliged, I'm sure!'

'Much obliged, I'm sure'? Had I suddenly turned into Eliza Doolittle, or a 1920s housemaid called Ethel? Why couldn't I ever just be *cool*? Not like cool as in wearing the latest clothes and knowing the right bands, but just cool as in sophisticated and elegant and witty? Or failing that, couldn't I just be *normal*?

On the plus side, it didn't rain.

EMILY

CHAPTER ELEVEN

Wow. Lila was reprehensible, kissing Ben like that, low ebb or no low ebb!

Is slut-shaming OK if it's actually your mother? And it happened, like, a million years ago? I suspect Mum would say no, it was not OK to slut-shame her, and would probably make some excuse about how it was a long time ago and things were different in the nineties. Morals are morals, though, Lila. You can't just go around kissing whoever you like and claiming 'low ebbs'. We have all been at a low ebb, and snogging Welsh randoms, however nice their accent, or handsome they are when angry, is *not* the answer!

Also, this diary is meant to be helping me learn how I'm not the first person to have my heart broken, and so far, all that seems to happen is more people falling for Lila, which frankly I am not finding very cheering or helpful *at all*.

I woke up this morning with my face pressed against

the pages. There was a strange, sweet smell clinging to the diary, sort of like synthetic peaches, or the peach schnapps I had tasted at Poppy's house once when her mum and dad were out and her older sister gave us some to try. I wondered if Lila had spilled peach schnapps on the book, or if it was the remains of some forgotten nineties perfume. It was quite nice.

What had woken me up, though, was the sound of Dad and Stella having a massive row downstairs. I blearily looked at my phone. What was Stella even doing here at 8.30 a.m. on a Saturday morning? I tried to put the pillow over my head to drown out the shouting, but curiosity got the better of me. If they didn't want me to hear them, they should keep their voices down!

The argument, it turned out, was about how Stella had rocked up bright and early, armed with seeds, demanding Dad spend the day in the garden with her, repairing the damage I had wrought upon her 'babies'. Ugh, I hoped I wasn't going to be roped in too. Spending the day gardening with Stella was literally the last thing I wanted to do.

As I listened on, though, it turned out Dad shared my opinion, and had categorically said no, that he was taking me out for the day, for 'bonding'. Although I almost cringed myself inside out at Dad using phrases like 'bonding', and I hoped he wasn't going to be mega embarrassing about it all, even 'bonding' with Dad was preferable to spending the day with Long-Suffering Stella. A day that would probably end with lentil bake to round off the misery!

Dad was now yelling that Stella was being ridiculous, and his daughter was having a really hard time right now and she was only fourteen and she needed her father. Nearly fifteen, I thought indignantly. Why does everyone forget I'm *nearly fifteen* and insist on referring to me as only being fourteen?

'I need you, Andrew,' Stella shrieked. 'I am also having a very hard time, but you don't seem to care, you just always put her first, ahead of ME! It's not FAIR! When are you going to put ME first?'

'Grow up, Stella,' Dad bellowed. 'You sound like a whining teenager! I'm never going to put you before my daughter, because she's my DAUGHTER, and also at the moment she is still a child and she needs me.'

Rude, I thought. I am so not a child.

'And even when she's an adult, Stella, I will still put her first, because that's what parents do,' Dad carried on. 'I was upfront about that from the moment we met – that Emily will always come first, and I will never love anyone more than Emily. So if you've got a problem with that, or you can't understand what it *means* to be a parent, then maybe we need to rethink this relationship!'

Oooh, was he DUMPING Stella? Oh, hang on, Stella was still going.

'How DARE you say I don't understand what it means to be a parent!' she wailed. 'What about my PLANT BABIES that YOUR daughter murdered, like . . . like something out of *King Lear*!'

'Stella, some withered parsley is hardly comparable to a flesh-and-blood child. And Emily was just trying to be helpful.'

'And there you go again, taking her side.' Stella sounded like she was crying now. Serves her right for going around telling people I'm a murderer. 'I'm just asking for a little bit of your time and attention, Andrew. That's all.'

'You get ALL my time and attention while Emily is at Lila's –'

'And that's another thing. You never seem to be off the phone to Lila. What's going on there?'

'She's Emily's mother. We are worried about Emily. Naturally, WE NEED TO TALK TO EACH OTHER. BECAUSE WE SHARE A CHILD!'

'Emily, Emily, Emily!' shrieked Stella. 'All I hear about is Emily! I'm sick of Emily!'

'And I'm sick of you behaving like this, being jealous of a child!' Dad suddenly yelled. 'I think you should go, Stella, before one of us says something we really regret.

I'll call you in a few days when we've both had some time to calm down and think about things.'

There appeared to be some muffled protestations from Stella, then the front door slammed very hard and I heard Dad go into the kitchen and put the kettle on.

I decided I had better wait a decent amount of time before getting up, so I could pretend I hadn't heard the row. Obviously, if Dad was upset, I was sorry, but at the same time it had been nice to hear him saying he would always put me first and love me best. It was something I'd needed to hear. Also, if he had fallen out with Stella, I would be safe from the lentil bake for a few days. Even better, if I could keep them from reconciling before I went home, I could have a whole visit with Dad free from Stella's cooking and opinions.

I was sure I could come up with some strategy to achieve this. In films they're always getting rid of their fathers' horrible girlfriends. On the other hand, they usually get shot of the vile new girlfriend in order to get their mum and dad back together, and I don't even really remember mine *being* together so it would be quite strange. I mean, I wouldn't stop it happening, but I don't think I'd go out of my way to achieve it. Unlike keeping Stella off the scene!

I doom-scrolled TikTok aimlessly for half an hour, until I was too hungry to stay in bed. Downstairs, Dad was on his laptop, and he grinned at me when I came into the kitchen.

'I'm just doing an online shop!' he said. 'I've ordered steak and bacon and sausages and stinky cheese and *white bread* and all the other things Stella continuously tells me are bad for me and tries to stop me from eating!'

'Oooh, can you get ice cream?' I asked eagerly.

'Already in there. Three kinds.'

'Chocolate spread? Coco Pops?'

Dad tapped and said, 'Done!'

Meanwhile, I scoured the kitchen to find something nicer for breakfast than the home-made sugar-free granola Stella so kindly provided Dad with, because I'd finished the stash of mini packets of cereal he'd bought for my visit. At the back of a cupboard, I found a battered packet of Pop Tarts. Dad looked at them suspiciously and asked what the use-by date was, as he didn't even remember buying them and feared they might have been there since I was about six. I couldn't even read the use-by date, it had faded so much, but Dad shrugged in the end and said they were probably so full of E numbers that they would last forever.

'So have you broken up with Stella then? If you're buying all this stuff she doesn't let you have?' I asked Dad through a mouthful of Pop Tart.

Dad sighed and said it was complicated (why do

grown-ups always say this?), but things hadn't been great between Stella and him for a while, and didn't seem to be getting any better, so he didn't really see a future for them.

'Is it because of me that you're breaking up?' I asked. Although I had hated the thought that I might've been the reason Mum and Dad split up, I wasn't so sad about being the catalyst for Dad dumping Sanctimonious Stella.

'No,' said Dad quickly. 'No, we're just . . . too different, I think. Now what do you want to do today? We could go to the museum?'

I had last enjoyed a trip to the museum about the same time Dad bought those Pop Tarts. I tried my hardest to look enthusiastic, but I clearly didn't succeed, as Dad looked a bit disappointed and suggested going to an art gallery instead.

I wasn't mad on the idea of art galleries either, but I thought perhaps I should start trying to be more cultured and knowledgeable about things like art, if I wanted people to take me seriously and realise I am really very mature for my age, so I agreed that sounded like a good idea.

'And then,' Dad offered, 'we could always get some lunch and maybe go shopping?'

'What sort of shopping?' I needed to know before I agreed, in case he wanted to take me somewhere deathly boring like a garden centre, which would be full of plants and old people and weird soft furnishings.

'Well, I thought maybe I could get you some new clothes? Cheer you up a bit?' Dad said.

That was more like it. Though I wasn't convinced Dad's idea of suitable shops would be the same as mine. There was no point in new clothes if he was going to make me go to John Lewis, which is such an old person's shop, but Dad agreed he would let me choose whatever shops I wanted, within reason, providing they weren't too expensive.

It was a good day with Dad. We agreed neither of us really understood the 'art' in the art gallery, which was all very 'conceptual', but decided we were probably still better people for having nourished our souls with culture. Then we had pizza for lunch, and afterwards Dad turned me loose in Hollister. There was some disagreement on what I considered suitable clothing and what Dad did, but unlike Mum, I was able to persuade him that *literally everyone* wears stuff like this, and also, unlike Mum, I wore him down by just browsing the rails for ages until he lost the will to live and agreed to buy me anything I wanted as long as he could leave this dark, noisy, strange-smelling shop.

'I don't know about you, darling, but I'm exhausted,' groaned Dad, when we finally left the shop. 'I cannot be bothered cooking tonight, shall we be very extravagant and go out for dinner as well as lunch? There's a nice Italian place I've been wanting to try. Stella wouldn't go as there weren't enough vegan options. What do you say? You could even wear one of those new dresses you've just conned out of me.'

I agreed enthusiastically, so we went back to Dad's and got changed, and then walked to the restaurant which was quite fancy, and it felt like a proper treat night.

Dad talked to me like an adult instead of a child. He didn't say, 'Oh, Emily, really, spaghetti carbonara, can't you try something new for once?' and even let me have a few sips of his wine when no one was looking. I felt like I was becoming *extremely* mature and quite possibly no one would even recognise me when I went home, because I would be so sophisticated and far too cultured to bother with their backward ways.

While we were waiting for our tiramisu, I revised my fantasy about Oli seeing me and realising what a terrible mistake he had made in dumping me, and begging me to take him back, because in this version I simply laughed coldly and informed him that my mind was now on *far* higher things than the likes of Oliver Letby, or indeed any boys. I was devoting myself to the pursuit of knowledge and art and beauty, and I had no time for such nonsense. What bliss it would be if that happened!

Of course, I would be lying a bit, because I do still very

much want *someone* to fall in love with me. Even Lila had at least three boys in love with her when she was not very much older than I am. I gave a deep sigh as I wondered what Lila had that I don't.

'What's wrong, Emily?' asked Dad. 'You've looked miles away for the last five minutes, and now you're huffing and puffing. Didn't you enjoy your dinner?'

'No, I did.'

I tried not to sigh again, lest Dad think I was very ungrateful for the lovely day we had spent together. Maybe it was the sips of wine that he had given me, or how he'd been so nice to me and hadn't treated me like a child, but suddenly I felt I would try and talk to him.

'It's just . . . Lila's diary . . .' I began.

'How are you getting on with that?' Dad asked with interest. 'You have no idea how much I'm having to resist the temptation to sneak a look and see what she had to say about us all back then.'

I informed Dad with some dignity that that would be a *gross* invasion of Lila's privacy, not to mention my and Lila's trust, and he protested he hadn't had any intention of *actually* looking.

'But why is Lila's diary making you sigh over your dinner?' he asked again.

And then it all came rushing out.

'It's just . . . everyone seemed to fall in love with her. You. Nicky. A boy called Ben. No one has ever fallen in love with me, and I don't think they ever will. How do you get boys to like you?'

Dad took a very large slug of his wine when I said this, and asked a passing waiter to bring him another glass of red before he finally said, 'You . . . um . . . just be yourself?'

'That's what everyone says!' I stormed. '*Just be yourself.* That's such rubbish advice. Boys don't want me to be myself. They want girls who look like the girls on the internet. With lip filler, and big boobs and bums, and long blonde hair. That's all they're interested in. And I don't look like that, and I probably never will because Mum gives me massive lectures about how dangerous fillers are and why I shouldn't get a boob job when I'm older and cosmetic surgery is just a tool of the patriarchy to oppress women into a stereotypical ideal of beauty and all that stuff, but I just want someone to notice me! To like me! To fall, just a little bit, in love with me. But they never will, and all anyone says is, "Just be yourself!" I don't *want* to be myself. I want to be someone better!'

'Thank you!' Dad said gratefully to the waiter who had placed another glass of wine in front of him, from which he took another huge gulp as I blinked back tears.

'Want another sip?' he offered, and I nodded gratefully

and took as big a mouthful as I could. It wasn't nearly as nice as the peach schnapps Poppy's sister gave us, but Dad was trying to help, and trying to make me feel like more of an equal, so I didn't want to say no, and also it seemed to be helping him with this conversation, so I thought maybe it would help me too. But it just made me feel a bit dizzy.

'Emily,' Dad finally said. 'I know teenage boys are shallow creatures driven by the contents of their trousers –'

'DAD!'

'And I know the internet has changed things a lot, but even when I was young, yes, we *fancied* the girls with the big boobs and the pouty lips and the blonde hair, but they weren't necessarily the girls we fell in love with, or at least not *just* because of how they looked. But boys . . . men – we fall for girls who make us laugh, who we feel like we can talk to, who interest us. There's more to love than sex.'

Dad gave me a stern look as I opened my mouth to protest again. 'No, Emily, if you want to be treated like an adult, you should be able to cope with your father saying that word. I know this boy has hurt you very much, and his behaviour has left you questioning your worth, and there's no excuse for how he treated you. The way teenage boys carry on often makes me want to apologise to all of womenkind on behalf of men, given we were all teenage boys once. But none of that is a reflection on you.'

'It's not?' I said in a small voice.

Dad shook his head. 'If this boy dumped you because he wanted someone to have sex with, like your mother seems to think, it doesn't make you less in any way. It just means he's letting himself be ruled by his basest instincts. And he may yet grow up to become a perfectly decent man who feels ashamed of how he behaved at sixteen, or he may just be a terrible specimen of the male species, but *none* of that is *anything* to do with you.'

Dad held up his hand again as I tried to interrupt.

'I'm not finished,' he said. 'Someone will fall in love with you, I promise. Not because you're beautiful, though you are, but because under the anger and teenage angst and attitude, you are an incredibly kind and funny girl. And once boys get over the obsession with boobs and bums, which is probably something primal to do with when we were monkeys, that's what they're looking for. That's why I fell in love with Lila, and so did Nicky and Ben.' He laughed suddenly. 'God, I haven't thought about Ben in years until you mentioned him the other night!' Then he looked at me. 'Do you understand what I'm trying to say, Emily, darling?'

I nodded. Dad hadn't really said anything earth-shattering that Mum hadn't tried to say to me already, but somehow it made more sense coming from someone who had once been a teenage boy himself, hearing that there might be hope for me yet.

Of course, Dad was biased, and had to say nice things about me, because that's what dads do, but it was good to hear that maybe I wasn't entirely unlovable. And that there are boys out there who aren't just After One Thing. But how did I *find* one? And how would I feel when I went back to school and saw Oli again? It was all very well spending the summer here with Dad and trying to reinvent myself and imagining all the cutting put-downs I would *wither* Oli with when I next encountered him, but it might be another thing all together when I actually had to be near him. What if he still made my tummy flip, and those butterflies flutter in my heart? Just because I knew he was an awful person, didn't mean I was over him.

Dad must've read my mind, because he said, 'Emily, when you *do* fall in love, properly in love, with someone who deserves you, I promise it will feel quite different to the teenage butterflies and stomach churning. When you do find the right person, they will be someone you don't feel you need to change who you are for, and you won't want to change them either.'

'Like Stella is trying to change you?' I asked.

Dad looked slightly rueful and laughed. 'Out of the mouths of babes. Yes, I suppose like Stella is trying to change me, and if I am honest, there are a lot of things about her I'd like to change too.'

'What about with Mum?' I wanted to know. 'Did you want to change her?'

Dad shook his head. 'No, not at first. At first, I was just so happy to be with her. But then, as time went on, I wanted her to love me more. And while I do believe she did love me, I don't think I was the person she really wanted, deep down. And so things started to go wrong.'

He paused and had a drink. 'Because that's the other thing, Emily,' he said. 'Love *changes*. All the time. If you're lucky, it changes for the better, and grows and deepens. And then you get to grow old with the love of your life. But sometimes it doesn't change into a better love. It changes into resentment, or anger, or even just indifference. And then it's not love any more.'

'But how do you know which it's going to be?' I asked.

'You don't. You just have to hope,' Dad said. 'And if it goes wrong, hope that it works out better next time. Because that's the other thing. For most people, there is not just one perfect love. There are lots of imperfect loves instead.'

Wow. That sounded like hard work.

'So you and Mum were an imperfect love?' I asked.

'We were,' Dad said. 'But that imperfect love gave us

something great. It gave us the thing we love most in the world – you!'

♡❤

I spent a lot of time thinking about what Dad had said. Even after the weekend when he made me go into work with him again and finish sorting out that stupid 'card index', which took me all of Monday and Tuesday, I turned over his comments in my mind, while he shouted at me to keep my drinks away from his precious cards, and I pointed out I had a right to adequate hydration and he was probably contravening my human rights. But finally, I felt a bit of hope that though Oli clearly wasn't the one, someone would fall in love with me one day, and that even if things didn't work out with one person, there was always the chance that the next time it would.

I wondered if that's what had happened to Lila. It hadn't worked with Nicky, but it had with Ben? Except, of course, it couldn't have worked with him either, or she wouldn't have married Dad, and that also had come to an end, and now she was on her own. Was she still looking for that perfect someone?

LILA

CHAPTER TWELVE

SUNDAY 2ND NOVEMBER 1997

I barely slept last night, I was so racked with guilt about Nicky and Ben. How could I have done that? How could I have kissed Ben, thus betraying Nicky *and* leading Ben on at the same time?

I am lower than a worm. I do not like feeling lower than a worm, and I do not know what I can possibly do to rectify this situation. Should I tell Nicky what happened? Should I apologise again to Ben?

I rang Jas and begged her to come over straight away so we could work out a plan of action. She was there within ten minutes, although she looked a little smirky when I asked how it had gone with Dan Wilcox last night, and she agreed she was definitely over her Man-Hating Phase.

I told her I had kissed Ben. Or rather, Ben had kissed me, and I had let him. And kissed him back. 'I am a worm, Jas,' I told her. 'I am lower than a worm.

What about Nicky?'

Jas immediately assured me that I was absolutely *not* a worm, and such a thing could literally happen to anyone, and also, she pointed out, I had been at a low ebb, which is *exactly* what I had thought myself last night! I was at a very low ebb indeed when Ben kissed me!

'So it's really not your fault at all, is it?' Jas said in a very reasonable tone. And she went on to say that if it was anyone's fault, it was Ben's for kissing me. And also, she put some of the blame on Nicky, because I hardly hear from him, so really, he put me at the low ebb, and Ben just happened to be there, when I was low ebbing.

'You are not even *slightly* wormy,' she concluded. 'You are the one who has been wronged.'

I said I might be a tiny bit worm adjacent, because I didn't *feel* very wronged. In fact, I had rather enjoyed kissing Ben. A bit too much, in all honesty. If I hadn't felt so terribly guilty about Nicky, I'd have enjoyed it even more. Jas said that was all fine, it was perfectly natural, and maybe more of the blame was Nicky's, for causing the low ebb, than Ben's for happening along in the ebbness.

I was immensely cheered to discover I could in no way be held accountable for last night, but it did not solve the other pressing concern. Should I tell Nicky about Ben kissing me? I could probably leave out the bit about me enjoying it, but still, I'm technically going out with Nicky and I've kissed – been kissed by – someone else.

Jas was adamant that I absolutely should not breathe a word about it to Nicky. What possible good could it do? He was all the way over there in Ohio, and if he didn't want to break up with me, it would only hurt him.

But what if he did want to break up with me? I pointed out that at least if I told him, we'd both know where we stood.

Jas still thought it was a bad idea. She pointed out that we had been at the end of that massive garden, so no one could possibly know what happened apart from me and Ben. And her. 'And I'm not going to say anything,' she finished.

'What if Ben tells people and someone tells Nicky?' I whimpered.

Jas advised that the best course of action in such a circumstance was denial. If Ben was so ungentlemanly as to kiss and tell, he deserved to look stupid if I said he had invented the whole thing. And who was Nicky going to believe – me, or some boy he had never even met?

I was doubtful of Jas's logic. It still felt wrong. Honesty was the best policy, wasn't it? I didn't want to keep secrets from Nicky. Jas persuaded me, though, that there was nothing to *tell* Nicky, because it wasn't my fault.

Eventually I accepted the wisdom of her argument. She was right, what good could possibly come of telling Nicky about last night? Especially when it really, really wasn't my fault!

Jas approved, and then said she needed to go, because Dan had rung and asked her to go for a coffee and was coming to meet her. 'Will you be OK?' she asked me.

I promised that yes, I would be fine now, and I was lucky to have such a sensible friend.

As I opened the door to say goodbye to Jas, I was astonished to see Ben coming up the path with Dan. Jas widened her eyes at me in surprise, and all I could do was shrug – I had no more idea what he was doing here than she did. We hadn't exactly parted on good terms.

'I'll call you later,' I whispered. 'And tell you what happens.'

Jas nodded, and skipped off merrily with Dan as I stared after her, envious of how simple their love life was compared to mine.

'Lila?' Ben said, and I realised that wasn't the first time he had said it. I pulled myself together and attempted to give him a friendly smile – but not too friendly.

Ben asked if he could come in and said he wanted to talk.

I nodded and stood aside to let him in, as Mum came

out of the kitchen. 'Oh,' she said. 'It's you again. You're here a lot, aren't you?'

'Mum,' I hissed. 'Shuddup!'

Of course, Mum did not shut up. She never does when I want her to. Instead she gave us both one of her Looks and then started going on about how she was just *saying* that this young man seemed to be here a lot, and did that mean things were over with poor Nicholas. I longed for the floor to open up and swallow me, but Mum was not done yet, as she carried on talking as if Ben wasn't standing RIGHT THERE, saying she hoped I hadn't had my Head Turned just because This Boy could drive. I knew exactly what people meant when they talked about burning with mortification. The embarrassment and shame she was currently causing me was a white-hot heat searing through my soul and my stomach. I actually thought I might be sick on the floor if she didn't shut up soon.

'Ben, come through here,' I snarled, glaring at Mum, who was still wittering at me as I tried to drag Ben into the sitting room.

Mum could not let me do anything as simple as use the sitting room, though, complaining that she needed to use the computer to email her sister Lucy about what to get their mother for Christmas. 'She says the only thing she needs is a new girdle, but I just don't feel that's very festive, do you?' I did not want to discuss the festiveness or otherwise of my grandmother's girdles in the hall with Ben standing there. In fact, I did not ever want to discuss my grandmother's girdles, festive or not, with anyone at all. Ever.

Instead, I attempted to usher Ben upstairs, before Mum asked his opinion on octogenarian undergarments, but Mum had not quite finished the wholesale humiliation she had evidently decided was the order of the day, and reminded me that I wasn't allowed boys in my bedroom, except of course for Nicky, since he was such a nice boy, according to Mum, that she knew wouldn't try any 'funny business'.

'Oh, how little you know, Mother,' I muttered under my breath. She would be astonished at how inventive *Such A Nice Boy* as Nicky could be.

Eventually she conceded I could take Ben into the kitchen. As long as I left the door open. I shoved Ben through the kitchen door as fast as I could, to get him away from Mum, who was clearly in One Of Those Moods, before she could say any more.

'He may have a cup of tea,' Mum called graciously after us.

I plonked Ben down at the kitchen table and turned to put the kettle on. Too late, I realised I had sat him with a clear and uninterrupted view into the utility room, where Mum had just helpfully hung all my bras and knickers on a clothes horse. Why, today of all days, had she decided to do that, instead of doing what she usually does and yelling at me to hang everything up to dry? Life (and Mum) was treating me most unfairly today.

I hastened across the kitchen and slammed the door closed, but I fear Ben had already had an eyeful of greying M&S knickers. To my (yet more) shame, all colours of my knickers were now greying, the black ones were fading and the white and coloured ones had all ended up in a dark wash at some point and were now also varying shades that could best be described as 'murk'.

My everyday bras alas were not in much better condition. I didn't know whether it was a good thing or a bad thing that my best Wonderbra and Good Pants (black lace, Knickerbox) were currently lying on my bedroom floor where I had flung them off last night (the rules of decent behaviour dictating that one must wear better pants to social occasions such as parties, even if no one is going to see them). I mean, obviously I didn't *want* Ben to see my sexier undies, but at the same time, I didn't want him to think I only owned grubby yet stoutly gusseted rags for undergarments.

I didn't want *anyone* to think that, I reminded myself,

not just Ben. Ben was nothing to me. As my pants should be to him.

At this point, utility room door firmly slammed, I gave serious consideration to simply collapsing on the floor and bursting into tears. Everything was too much. Last night had been too much. The guilt and lack of sleep had been too much. Mum's censorious behaviour when I hadn't even done anything wrong (well, *very* wrong, anyway) was too much. And even though Jas had nearly convinced me that I had nothing to feel guilty about, and everything was fine, now Ben was here in front of me, I did feel very guilty.

Guilty about the kissing.

Guilty about Nicky.

Guilty about how I couldn't help but notice how very, *very* handsome Ben was.

And worst of all, guilty about the little part of me that really wanted him to stand up from the table and stride manfully across the kitchen and sweep me into his arms before declaring his undying love for me and insisting that he must have me now (not literally, that would be unhygienic in a kitchen – just, you know, I must metaphorically be his).

Part of that fantasy was almost certainly a direct result of the wet week Mum and I had spent in Anglesey in the summer, where I had finished the books I brought on day two and there was very little else to do for the rest of the time except read my way through the shelves and shelves of Mills and Boon, which always ended with the hero striding manfully, sweeping up the heroine, declaring love, etc. before a chaste yet passionate kiss drew the book to a close. I had quite liked the sound of that. I had attempted to persuade Nicky to do some manful striding and sweeping up when we got home, but he had laughed and said did I realise life wasn't a Mills and Boon book, and anyway, I knew he loved me, so it would hardly be a dramatic revelation.

I had tried to console myself with the memory of the first time Nicky kissed me, last Christmas, which was the most achingly romantic moment of my life – even more romantic than anything I could have imagined, and I had imagined some *pretty* romantic scenarios. But there was something very Mills and Boon hero-esque about Ben that just made me think of the striding and sweeping – especially after last night and the way his handsomeness increased the crosser he got. In fact, it was all a bit Mr Darcy. I briefly wondered what Ben would look like wading out of a lake in a wet white shirt.

I told myself to get a grip. Things were awkward enough as they were without me starting on Mr Darcy fantasies about Ben. Though he did look a little bit like Colin Firth.

I attempted the Just Friendly and Nothing More smile at Ben again and he looked nonplussed. Was it too much? Was my friendly smile more of a seductive, come hither pout? Is that why he had kissed me last night, because all the time I thought I was giving him friendly smiles, I was in fact leering suggestively at him? I immediately stopped smiling and looked stern instead. There would be no mixed messages here!

'Have you got toothache, Lila?' asked Ben.

Toothache? Did I *look* like I had toothache? I was quite put out, though also relieved that I hadn't been casting smouldering looks his way, and so once again, I could not possibly be blamed for last night.

Trying not to do the toothache face, I assured him I was fine and offered him a cup of tea and a Rich Tea biscuit. Very good, Lila, I congratulated myself. Rich Tea biscuits are the dullest, worst, most pointless biscuits known to humanity. No one being offered a Rich Tea biscuit could be in any doubt about the virtuous intentions of the offerer. Now a Hobnob would be a very different story. One could land oneself in all manner of hot waters with a delicious HobNob. Rich Teas, though, were quite safe. Practically a Victorian-style chaperone in baked-goods form!

'No, thanks,' said Ben. 'Just the tea, please.'

Ha! I had successfully thwarted any nefarious intentions

Ben may have been harbouring through the medium of Rich Tea biscuits. That is, if he was a) harbouring any in the first place, and b) Mum and my greying underwear and my toothache face had not already killed said intentions.

I made us both a cup of tea and brought them over to the kitchen table. Unfortunately, I tripped over my fashionably very flared jeans on the way to the table – something Mum had been insisting was an accident waiting to happen ever since I proudly bore them home from Topshop a couple of weeks ago. I stumbled and almost fell, managing to right myself, but not before I had hurled two mugs of scalding tea right smack into Ben's crotch.

Ben screamed. I wailed. He leaped to his feet as the burning liquid soaked through to his most very delicate gentleman's area and I grabbed a tea towel and attempted to minister to his parboiled bits. A still whimpering Ben wrenched down his jeans in an attempt to alleviate the pain.

It was at this *most* inopportune moment that Jas burst through the back door, shouting, 'LILA! I forgot my – OH!'

She stopped stock-still at the sight of Ben in his pants in the middle of my kitchen and me patting at his mid-section and immediately shot straight back out the door. Though not before Dan Wilcox, following her, had also been party to this very unfortunate scenario.

Just as Jas and Dan exited again, Mum dashed in through the kitchen door demanding to know what all the noise was about, couldn't she even get five minutes' peace to send an email on a Sunday morning? Ben, beetroot in the face with pain and / or embarrassment, tried to cover himself up, while Mum furiously enquired what he thought he was doing and to *put his trousers on immediately and get out*. I explained I might actually have accidentally caused third-degree winkle burns, and Ben whimpered he didn't even think he could put his trousers on, it hurt too much.

At that point, Mum switched into doctor mode. She ordered me out of the room, and told Ben to take his pants off as well and run *everything* under the cold tap while she assessed the damage.

In the hall, I heard Mum snapping, 'No, *right* under the tap. Yes, like that! Thank goodness Lila washed up the breakfast dishes when she was meant to!' as I sank to the floor with a groan of misery. The best-looking boy in college was currently half naked in my kitchen, with his unmentionable bits in the sink, under the eagle-eyed supervision of *my mother*. How did these things happen to me? Was he going to be all right? Even if he was not physically scarred, surely he would be mentally traumatised for life by the experience? I know Mum is a doctor and well used to seeing all sorts of body parts, and would say people shouldn't be so silly – to a doctor even intimate areas are no more interesting or exciting than a toe or a nose – but I doubt Ben will feel like that.

I crawled up to my room and into bed, hoping I could simply die of mortification. I hid under the covers, waiting for the sound of the front door slamming to signify Ben's departure. But of course, how could he leave when he didn't have any dry trousers to wear? Assuming he could even put a pair of trousers on again and wasn't too *maimed*.

Eventually, I heard Mum come up the stairs, and I pulled the duvet even tighter over my head.

'Come out of there, Lila,' she said in a tone that brooked no argument.

I tentatively poked my head out and looked at her in trepidation, unsure if I was in for the lecture to end all lectures, or the news that I had melted Ben into some sort of Ken-doll arrangement Down There.

Mum informed me that 'my friend' – she made the word *friend* sound quite sordid – had explained what had happened. There then followed a lecture about how she had *told* me those jeans were dangerous, etc, before she finally gave me the good news that Ben would be fine, that the trousers off and cold water had done the trick and his mother was on her way to collect him, bearing dry clothes.

'You can go down and see him while he's waiting for her.' Mum said magnanimously.

'I can't,' I groaned, pulling the duvet back over my head. 'It's too awful. You're my mother and you've seen his *thingy*! How can I face him now?'

'Really, Lila,' Mum was at her most doctorly brisk, 'the word is *penis* –'

'Arrrrgghhhhh!' I gave a muffled shriek.

There obviously followed another lecture about how if I wasn't mature enough to hear words like 'penis' then I wasn't mature enough to have a boyfriend, whether that was Nicholas or the unfortunate boy sitting in the kitchen in one of her John Lewis towels. She went on for some time in that vein, while all I could think was 'please never let me have to hear my mother say the word "penis" ever again'. It seemed the only way to stop her was to get out of bed and go downstairs.

'And do something about those STUPID TROUSERS of yours before you or someone else is SERIOUSLY injured!' she shouted after me as I shuffled out the door.

Ben was sitting in the kitchen, still a funny shade of puce. At this point I wasn't sure if he was now scarlet with embarrassment, pain or heat, but from my own point of view, I was at least relieved to see that Mum had given him one of the good towels, and not one of my ancient, threadbare My Little Pony ones, which I wouldn't have put past her.

'Hi,' I mumbled, not quite able to look him in the eye.

'Hi,' he mumbled back, also keeping steadfast eye contact with the scratched surface of the kitchen table.

I made vaguely apologetic noises, which I very much hoped conveyed my deep and abiding regret about my attempt to frazzle his frankfurter.

Ben made equally vague noises and fixed his gaze somewhere near the kitchen clock.

I wondered if I should offer him a cup of tea, then I saw him glance at the kettle and wince, so I decided against it. The silence was too awkward and I couldn't bear it. I considered just running out the door and abandoning the whole excruciating situation, but I feared Mum would be lurking in the hall, poised to shove me back into the kitchen and telling me to *grow up*. The back door then? I cast a hopeful glance in its direction. I could be out the door and down the road before Mum even heard it close!

Come on, Lila, I said sternly to myself. Where would you go after that? You'll still have to come home and face your mother at some point, not to mention Ben at college tomorrow. Perhaps I could go and live with Kate and Kevin? They had a huge house. I could probably sneak in and live in one of their bedrooms and they wouldn't even notice I was there! I could scavenge in their enormous kitchen at night for fancy yogurts and branded cereal, and drink iced water from the big, magic American fridge that had a little cubby hole that dispensed delicious cold water. During the day, when they were out, I could do secret helpful acts around the house, like a sort of daytime *Elves and the Shoemaker* scenario. I could be there for years, and no one would ever know.

Except Mum would probably insist on calling the police if I was last seen fleeing down the road from a boy wrapped in a peach cotton bath towel and an Oasis T-shirt and I never returned. No doubt there would be a tremendous fuss. And imagine if they started searching my friends' houses, which for all I know might be a thing that happens, and I was found asleep in Kevin's third-best spare room, soundly snoozing under his Laura Ashley duvet cover? I would *literally* never live it down and might as well just die of shame on the spot. Would that make Kevin an accessory to murder? I could not risk poor Kevin going to prison on my account. I would just have to face up to things.

I took a deep breath and reminded myself I was doing this to save Kevin from languishing in a grey stone prison cell, his only friend a curious rat, his only sustenance a dry crust and some stale water. You are *practically* Sydney Carton, going to the scaffold to save another in *A Tale of Two Cities*, I told myself.

'It is a far, far better thing I do . . .' I muttered to myself, and Ben gave me an odd look.

Then, 'Look, about last night –' we both said in unison and then stopped and looked at each other sheepishly.

Ben started talking first, saying he had come over to say sorry for last night, for getting his wires crossed and that he would like it if we could forget it all ever happened and just still be friends.

I said of course, and I was sorry too, and maybe we could also forget about the whole boiling liquids in the lap thing, which I was also very sorry about.

So we were both very sorry, and then Ben's mum arrived, shrieking, 'Oh, my poor Ben-Ben baby, did your Mr Winky get burned? Are you sure you're OK? Do you need a wet flannel for it?'

I was very relieved it's not just my mother who is utterly embarrassing in public, and Ben once again looked like he wanted the ground to swallow him up. While Mrs Morgan glared at me – the clumsy oaf who had tried to deprive her of grandchildren – Ben was ushered out to the car (walking rather gingerly, despite Mum's hearty insistences that he was 'right as rain' and that everything was 'tickety-boo'). Then Mum stomped off to the sitting room to '*finally*' email Aunt Lucy about Granny's Christmas undergarments, and I was on my own again at last.

The first thing I did, obviously, was to ring Jas, to clarify that whatever she *thought* she might have seen in the kitchen earlier was in fact perfectly innocent. She was still out with Dan, so I left a message with her mum to call me back *immediately* when she got home. I stressed the urgency several times, so Mrs Chatterjee was a little curt about it, telling me she did understand what 'very important' and 'right away' meant, though as she put the phone down I heard her say, 'Though I think we might have slightly different definitions of "very important",' which was rude.

I made a cup of tea (very carefully) and read *Cosmo* for a bit, while I thought about the conversation with Ben. Obviously, it was the best possible outcome. But a small part of me was slightly put out that he'd given up so soon. I took a *Cosmo* 'Does He Fancy Me?' quiz with Ben in mind, and it came out that he *definitely* fancies me. Not that I want him to, of course, it's much better that he just wants to be friends. But part of me rather liked the idea of him fancying me and how very much it would infuriate Rachel. It was the same nasty part of me that had slightly wished that Rachel could somehow know that *I* had snogged Ben last night and *she* hadn't.

Sometimes I worry that I'm not a very good person.

Then I remembered how I had nobly saved Kevin

from prison earlier, with no thought to my own personal comfort, so probably I'm not that terrible.

After my tea and *Cosmo* time, I decided, now everything was cleared up with Ben, that I could write to Nicky with a clear conscience. I know I had resolved no more letters, only emails, but maybe I just needed to write him a nice long chatty letter, funny and gossipy and maybe a tiny bit flirty, without being too try-hard and needy and stressing my undying love for him in every sentence. The sort of letter that will make him laugh, and remind him that he misses me, and hopefully give him a nudge towards actually *communicating* with me again. A letter so fabulous, in short, that it cannot be unreplied to.

It took me all afternoon to finish the letter, with a short break on the phone to Jas to explain the whole Ben / no trousers incident. She assured me she would set Dan straight on the matter as well, and pointed out that she'd been right all along and nothing was my fault. Then Mum yelled I had been on the on the phone for over an hour and phone bills, which was *very* unfair, as Jas had called *me*.

I posted the letter, and then came home and sent Nicky a short email about the party, like I had promised to, and had a reasonably nice dinner with Mum, if you don't count her grumbling *again* about the phone bill, though I reminded her once more that Jas had called *me*, and then

I went to bed, to sleep the sound sleep of the innocent and guiltless, which I was in sore need of, since I had had almost no sleep the night before because I was worrying so much.

EMILY

CHAPTER THIRTEEN

Dad and I came home at lunchtime today, as I pointed out I had already slaved half the week for him, and Thursday is *practically* the weekend. Dad claimed I had said that last week on Friday, and my weekends seemed to be getting longer and longer, but he agreed we could leave early. He did have some emails to catch up on first, though, and rudely suggested that I perhaps refrain from gardening, or anything else I considered would be 'helpful'.

There is still no word from Poppy, and she has not resurfaced on Life360, even though I can see everyone else in our circle on there, so I am forced to assume it is not a satellite-based disaster causing her disappearance, but rather that she doesn't want anything at all to do with me. To take my mind off this, I read a bit more of the diary while Dad did his emails and made dinner.

Poor Ben. I don't know the boy, of course, but I *do* know Granny MacKay, and I can just imagine how mortifying it must have been for him to have her dealing with his scalded bits. And how funny that Mum, who now reproaches me, Granny MacKay style, for being too immature to say things like 'penis' and 'vagina', was once also too prudish to say them. Though even I haven't stooped to the depths of calling a boy's parts a 'frankfurter'! Frazzled or otherwise.

I could just see Oli's face if I said something like that. He used much cruder words than 'frankfurter' for describing such areas, which had always slightly given me the ick, if I was perfectly honest with myself. I wished I had said so, though at the time I had quashed any such notions and told myself it was not *possible* for someone like Oli to give anyone the ick.

It felt quite empowering to realise that I was increasingly thinking about Oli with scorn and judgement, instead of longing and misery spiked with embarrassment.

Was it feasible that I was getting over him at last?

There had been quite a lot of occasions, really, when I didn't feel comfortable with the things Oli and his friends would say, especially about women, or some of the TikTokkers they liked to watch – a lot of them were very problematic men. And the jokes they would tell that I didn't quite get but somehow knew I'd be ashamed about if Mum saw me laughing along.

I've realised I don't think I ever actually liked Oli for

himself. I really had just been dazzled that a slightly older and extremely popular boy was interested in *me*, boring little Emily Osbourne. If I was completely honest, that had been Oli's only attraction. Not his wit (crass), his charm (dubious), his personality (challenging), his style (see charm), or even his looks (OK, he was very good-looking, which I suspect is why despite the other considerable defects, he was still very popular), just the reflected glory I could bask in, as the sort of girl that someone as popular as Oli Letby would be interested in. And so I was forced to conclude that it was indeed my pride that was wounded, rather than my heart.

I *hate* it when Mum is right. It's *so* unfair. Like, she has *much* more life experience than me, so obviously she stands a much higher chance of being right about things, and there's no need for her to be so smug about it, when it's not even because she's so very clever or morally superior, she just has a greater empirical chance of being right, because she is very, very OLD!

I pointed that out to Mum once. It didn't end well.

I have been so stupid. How could I have let my head be turned by such a shallow, foolish creature as Oli Letby? More to the point, how could I have fallen out with Poppy, the best friend anyone could ever hope for, over that idiot?

The closeness between Lila and Jas in Lila's diary made

me miss Poppy more than ever. Just like Jas always had Lila's back, so Poppy always had mine. When Oli left me in floods of tears outside the school disco – who was there with tissues and sympathies and hugs and fierce whispers of, 'He's so not worth it'? Who is the person who can always make me laugh, however bad things are? Who do I share my darkest secrets and most joyous hopes with?

Not Oli. I don't think I ever had more than the most superficial level of conversation with him.

And who did I turn on, and push away and say terrible things to, because she dared to give Grace Walker the time of day – Grace, who I decided was public enemy number one, just because Oli had declared his intention to pursue her, and who I knew nothing about at all, least of all whether Oli's advances had been accepted, and yet who I had chosen to ruin my friendship with Poppy over? Poppy, the most important person in my life apart from Mum and Dad. Poppy, who I always envisaged would be there forever, Poppy and me, laughing and reminiscing over glasses of wine when we are as old as Mum and Auntie Jas. Poppy, who is supposed to be *my* Jas.

I still wasn't buying Lila's low ebb excuse, nor was I one hundred per cent convinced that kissing Ben and betraying Nicky was in no way Lila's fault, but I was in no position to judge, as Lila had not done anything as terrible as me. Ben and Nicky were only boys. Stupid, *stupid* boys. They didn't *matter*. What mattered was *friends*. Lila and Jas and Kate and Tom had always been true to each other, and still were. Like I should have been to Poppy. How could I have been so selfish, and so mean? To my *best friend*? And over *Oli Letby*?

My whole body felt scorchingly hot every time I thought about Poppy. And the more I tried not to think about Poppy, the more I thought about Poppy and the more it burned. Perhaps I had a terrible illness? Fever, some sort of dreadful fever! Perhaps the clothes in H&M had been imported through some exotic port and one of my dresses had somehow picked up a vicious disease-carrying insect and it had bitten me and even now I was dying of scarlet fever or ebola. Maybe not ebola, I think it involves a lot of vomiting and diarrhoea and mostly I just had the burning, so definitely scarlet fever.

I flopped on to my bed with a feeble moan as I googled the symptoms.

No one responded to my feeble moan, so I moaned a little louder. Luckily Dad took his cue this time and came rushing up the stairs.

'Emily?' he said anxiously outside the door. 'Are you all right?'

'I think I have scarlet fever,' I whimpered.

Dad burst into my room as I thrust my phone at him, already on the NHS page for scarlet fever. 'You don't have a rash,' he objected, after briefly reading over the symptoms, 'and you've not had a sore throat. But perhaps I should ring your mother, just in case?'

I sat up bravely. 'No, don't call Mum. I'll be fine. Just, you know, felt a little scarlet fevery, that's all.'

Dad felt my forehead. 'I suppose you do feel a little warm,' he said doubtfully. 'Maybe just try to get an early night, eh?'

Ah, the good old 'early night', the grown-up cure for everything, along with 'drinking some water' and 'getting some fresh air' and 'seeing how you feel later'. It would serve them all right if one day I really *was* ill and was found close to death, asleep, well hydrated, in the fresh air, later. Ha!

My near-death experience (I have seen *Little Women*, I know the true fate of the scarlet-fever sufferers like Boring Beth) had made me see one thing clearly. I could not allow this situation with Poppy to continue one minute longer. I had caused it, so I had to fix it. Even if that meant backing down and admitting I was wrong. I could not die while my fight with Poppy was unresolved.

Before I could over-analyse it, I quickly typed –

Poppy, I'm so sorry I was so wrong I don't hate you you're my best friend and I never should have said that you can be friends with whoever you want please forgive me though xx

I pressed send before I could change my mind and returned to Lila's diary to distract myself instead of checking my phone every twenty seconds to see if Poppy had read the message, or if the wavering dots of doom were suggesting she was typing a reply.

LILA

CHAPTER FOURTEEN

SATURDAY 8TH NOVEMBER 1997

It has felt like an endless week. I wish letters didn't take so *long* to get to America. Having posted my, frankly brilliant, letter to Nicky, I am finding it very hard to have to wait for a reply, or even just for him to get it and maybe send me an email in response. Just something like '*Dearest Lila, thank you for your amazing letter, I have been a rubbish boyfriend for not writing to you in the manner you deserve, and I am going to try much harder from now on because you are the best girlfriend in the world and I love you . . .*' Then maybe something about how pretty I am (I know I'm not stunningly gorgeous like Kate, but hopefully in Nicky's eyes I scrub up OK) and perhaps a bit about how he can't live without me, etc., etc. A comparison of my complexion to a blushing summer rose might be nice. Though unlikely. Nicky is the sweetest boy in the world, but has a tendency to take things a bit literally, and also to offer scientific explanations for things I want to find achingly tender romantic reasons for. Like when I wanted to wish on a shooting star and he painstakingly explained it wasn't a star at all, it was a meteor, and it had no light of its own, it was just a piece of rock, lit up from the heat when it collided with the air in the Earth's atmosphere. Like, way to ruin a moment, Nicky!

He does have a romantic streak, though, really. How could I forget the way he brought me the first rose from his mother's garden every year, for as long as I can remember? And all the little things he'd done for Mum and me, even though until recently I took him for granted as just the weird boy next door? He didn't mind that I called him Weird Nicky to his face, even though Mum always told me off. Whenever I needed him, he had always been there, to help me, to have my back, which was all worth far more than poems and flowery words.

If only he was still next door, life would be so much easier. And if only there were some sort of words from him. *Any* words. Not flowery ones, just more than a sentence or two indicating how he is feeling! There wasn't even a reply to my cheery email about Kate's fireworks party. Maybe I should have said the fireworks had been terrible, without him helping Kevin to set them off, instead of how good they were. Perhaps he has taken umbrage. I suppose it was a bit tactless. But I had promised to email him about the party, and since there was quite a bit that I *couldn't* tell him about, I'd tried to focus on the good parts and be positive and make it sound fun, so he didn't think anything had happened.

By Wednesday I had tired of checking my email in every free period, and Mum had outright forbidden me logging on every hour at home. Imagine if you could just use the internet as much as you wanted, without parents there to complain you were bankrupting them by just *very quickly seeing* if the love of your life had got in touch! Mum is being particularly shirty about bills at the moment, so I can't even spend my evenings on the phone to Jas to distract me. Assuming Jas would even be there, as Dan Wilcox is now her Official Boyfriend.

Everyone seems loved-up, except me. Well, I AM loved-up, he's just not here! Jas and Dan are an item, Tom and Jon (so nearly rhymes, but probably just as well it doesn't), Kate and Matthew. Matthew is coming up again from Exeter this weekend to see Kate, and rings her every night, with no thought to *his* phone bill. Kate is starry-eyed, and although I'm thrilled for her, I wish Nicky would ring me, just once. I know Exeter and Ohio are very different when it comes to long-distance phone calls, and I know it is totally impractical, both for the cost and the time differences to expect him to phone, but I would so love to hear his voice.

And maybe in person, when we were talking, he could say all the things he seems unable to put into writing.

Not *everyone* is loved-up, I suppose. Andy and Luke aren't. Ben isn't either, of course, though Rachel is still pursuing him doggedly. At this point I genuinely don't know if I'd be relieved if he just gave in and got off with her in the middle of the cafeteria so I didn't have to feel guilty about him fancying me any more, or if I am still gleaning a nasty little bit of amusement that he is not that into Rachel because of me.

I must not think like that. Ben's romantic life is not my concern. In fact, I should be the Better Person and try to get him and Rachel together, now that Jas and Kate are spoken for. And yet, I cannot bring myself to do it. I know that the most annoying thing I could do to Rachel is be kind to her, but she has been so unremittingly vile to me (and Jas) since we were about seven that I just can't. Anyway, Ben is too nice for her, she'd only be horrible to him in the end, and it's not even as if she likes him for anything other than his looks anyway, so she doesn't deserve him.

This is definitely nothing to do with me hoping he could be a back-up plan if Nicky does turn out to have found some Miss All-American Star Cheerleader, because obviously should that happen, I will be swearing off men and devoting myself to Good Works forever.

In the meantime, while I wait for the Letter to arrive, I have decided to get on with things. No point in moping. Apart from anything else, my friends are sick of it, and they deserve better, especially now they've all found someone. So when Tom said Jon had the day off on Saturday, and he'd really like to meet us all, and why didn't we go for a coffee and then maybe a walk in the park since it was one of those lovely clear bright wintery days, with blue skies and crystalline air and crisp fallen leaves rustling under warm boots, and cosy scarves to snuggle into, I agreed. How could I not? I was damned if everyone else was going to hang out while I sat at home arguing with Mum about the phone bill!

Jon turned out to be *lovely*. And perfect for Tom. Where Tom is very obviously and classically good-looking, with his floppy dirty-blond hair and grey-blue eyes and chiselled jaw, Jon is handsome in the complete opposite way – dark and thin and intense with sexy glasses. He and Tom finish each other's poetry quotes and are so clearly besotted with each other that you can't even mind how pretentious they're being. It's lovely to see Tom so happy. No one deserves it more.

There was one slightly dicey moment when we decamped to the park. It was such a nice day that we ended up sitting on the grass, as by the time Kate and Matthew joined us, both rather flushed and sparkly-eyed, there were too many of us to sit on benches without looking ridiculous, all lined up in a row. Jas and Dan were wrapped around each other, Matthew had his arm slung around Kate, and I was sitting by Tom and Jon, who were holding hands, so I was trying very hard to not feel like a gooseberry.

Suddenly Tom gasped in horror. Bustling down the path towards us was his father. His old-fashioned, conservative, homophobic father.

Tom dropped Jon's hand and hissed, 'Put your arm around Lila, quick! Just do it!'

Jon looked confused, but did as he was told, so by the time Tom's dad reached us, there appeared to be three couples and a Tom-shaped gooseberry sitting on the grass.

Tom's father immediately barked at him, saying surely Tom had better things to do, like studying, than hanging round the park. Tom, with impressive thinking on his feet, quickly said we were all in a study group, just getting some fresh air while we took a quick break. His father looked entirely unconvinced and then demanded Tom should introduce him to his friends.

'Er, yes, of course. You know Kate, obviously, and this is Matthew, and Jas and Dan, and Lila and . . . Jon. This is my father, Richard Williams.'

'Hello, Mr Williams,' we all chorused politely.

Mr Williams looked us over disapprovingly, then turned to poor Tom again (he called him Thomas, which I had never heard anyone call him), tutting that it was a shame he couldn't get himself a nice girl too 'before people start thinking you're a homo'. We all tried not to gasp out loud in horror at that, as Mr Williams announced it had been nice to meet us, and gave us a curt nod and strode off.

Tom drooped on the grass, and Jon disentangled himself from me and grabbed his hand again. Tom mumbled apologies to Jon with tears in his eyes, as Jon hugged him and told him it was OK, he understood. Then we all quietly moved around Tom and Jon to screen them from the rest of the park, as Jon pulled Tom even closer and kissed him gently.

Later, Jon dropped Tom and me at my house. Mum was out on call, and we lay on the sofa watching *Dead Poets Society* for the hundredth time.

When we got towards the end, Tom paused it and asked me if I thought he was an awful coward for not standing up to his father, or telling him what Jon was to him.

Aghast, I promised him that neither I, nor any of our friends, could ever think that about him.

Tom was still sad, though, as he admitted that *he* thought he was a coward, for being so scared of his father, and how he would react if he knew Tom was gay.

I hugged Tom and pointed out that none of it was Tom's fault.

'You're not scared of who you are, you're scared of who he is, and I don't think he's a very nice person,' I said.

Tom was unconvinced, though, because his dad *is* still his dad, and it's so hard for Tom, having to hide who he is from his parents and from so many people at college. He wished more people were like Kate and Jas and me and the rest of our friend group, so he could be himself all the time. I wished the same too, as I told him that maybe things would change. Maybe in a few years, by the time our generation's children were the age we are now, it would be people like his dad who are judged and have to hide who they are. Or even better, no one will feel like that at all, and everyone can just be with whoever they want to be with!

Tom was still gloomy, though he said he was glad he had friends like me. Then he decided we needed to cheer up and discuss important topics like who was hotter – Keanu Reeves or Ethan Hawke? We argued for a while about how it depended what film they were in, and whether we were talking just to get off with, or forever, and Tom seemed cheerier when he left. But today put things in perspective. However bad things are for me, I don't think there's ever anything I would be too scared to tell my parents about.

They might shout and be disappointed and quite possibly ground me or punish me, depending on what I had done, but short of actually murdering someone in cold blood, I don't think there's anything that would make them say, 'We no longer love you, Lila, and you're not our daughter any more.'

Yes, Mum can be embarrassing, and yes, I suspect sometimes she does things purely to torment me for her own entertainment. And Dad – well. He's sad I'm not going to be a doctor, like MacKays are supposed to be, but he has never said he will not support me in my choices. Even Anita, who is far from the perfect stepmother, she too is perfectly accepting of who and what I am (i.e. not a Border terrier).

Tom puts on such a brave and happy and confident face for the world that it's easy to forget how alone and scared he must be sometimes. After all, it's one thing not being ready to come out to the whole college, but quite another to be afraid that your own parents won't accept you just because of who you love. I know it's not the same, but I hope we can give him enough love and support as his friends to help him through life, even if his parents can't.

I wish we were already grown-up and could do more to make the world a better place. If only we were adults, and people took us seriously, we could change attitudes and laws and *change the world*.

I said this once to Mum, and she looked at me quite oddly, and said that although she understood where I was coming from, to remember that I would never be as young again as I was in that moment, and the same was true for every minute that passed, and not to wish my youth away, however noble the cause, because I would only get one chance at youth, and one chance at life, so to make sure I made the most of both. There was no going back and doing it over. Every mistake we made, was made. You could atone, try to undo the damage, but you could never not do it. Likewise, every joyful moment, every wonderful thing, would only happen once. So be in the moment. Savour it. Enjoy it. Don't waste it on 'if onlys' and ways it could be better. Just live the one life you have, as best you can.

This was quite an impressive speech for Mum, who then cleared her throat and said talking of one life, did I think the laundry was going to bring itself in off the line, and to go and get it before it rained.

It's strange to think that there are no second chances at life, no waking up and saying, 'Oh no, hang on, I don't want to turn eighteen yet, I've done seventeen wrong, I need to go back and do it all again, get it right.' It's hard to wrap my head around there only being one time to be seventeen for me. Like there was one sixteen, one fifteen. Time never stops, and it only goes in one direction. But surely *we* will be young and seventeen forever? In the meantime, though, I must count my blessings and appreciate how lucky I am, and do my best to be a good person.

EMILY

CHAPTER FIFTEEN

This was a good distraction from Poppy's lack of reply to my message. But at the same time, I'm not sure it is the cheering distraction I had been hoping for. I needed more tales of the ridiculous scrapes Lila was capable of getting herself into. The whole entry was very sad, with the prejudices poor Uncle Tom faced, especially from his own father.

I had talked about this a bit with Uncle Tom at Easter. Thank goodness things are so much better now, and Uncle Tom is happy. He got divorced a couple of years ago, but Mum says apparently he has a lovely new boyfriend, though no one has met him yet – not because he's scared what people will think, but because, according to Uncle Tom, Mum and Auntie Jas and Auntie Kate can be 'A Bit Much Sometimes'. I know what he means, to be honest. I hope we all get to meet him soon, though, and they both live Happily Ever After!

I found Lila's musings about having only one chance to be young quite sobering and I lay awake half the night thinking about it. I was shattered this morning, and Dad said I did look a bit peaky, so I'd better stay at home. Obviously Mum says stuff like that to me all the time – 'Stop wishing your life away, Emily.' 'You've got plenty of time to grow up, Emily, enjoy being young while you can!' 'Don't be in such a rush to be an adult, Emily, it's not all it's cracked up to be' – but she's my mum and that's the sort of thing mums are *supposed* to say.

It was entirely different, reading it from seventeen-year-old Lila's point of view. I'd never thought about how I'm only going to be fourteen once. I've been so focused on wanting to be older that I've forgotten to enjoy just being fourteen.

Although I'm not entirely sure there's all that much *to* enjoy about being fourteen. To be honest, I'd prefer just to be four again, and in Reception, and have the biggest drama of the day be whether or not I got a chance to play in the house corner. Fourteen? Not so much. Fourteen is definitely what I overheard Mum describing to Dad on the phone as 'a very tricky age'. You're not a child, but you're not old enough to do anything really fun or interesting either. Seventeen would be much better. I can think of loads of reasons to regret never being seventeen again. And now

I'm doing it again – wishing I was older, even though I've not yet finished being fourteen, and like Lila said, I'll never be fourteen again.

And everything Lila was saying, about how you don't get the chance to rewind life and do things over? I think, deep down, I believed that was what could happen with Poppy, that somehow I could go back in time and change things, and we would never have that horrible fight, and I would be totally cool about her hanging out with Grace, and everything would be fine. But I realise now that's never going to be possible. The fight will always exist. I can't wave a magic wand and erase it. Maybe we can make up, maybe we will forget the summer we had such a terrible fight and I said such awful things, but I can't undo it. I can't undo anything. Everything that happens, stays happened.

I think on some level I have always just thought I was *practising* at life. That at best, this was a dress rehearsal, and once I found the right things to say, the right clothes to wear, the right sort of *person* to be, then I could put on the costume and someone would say, 'Curtain up,' and I would walk out on to the stage to play the word-perfect part of Emily Osbourne in *Emily's Life*. But there is no director to yell, 'CUT!' and say, 'Take two,' when things go wrong. There is only this. Unedited. Unfiltered.

How did I not know? How did Lila not know? Does

everyone have to find this out for themselves? Even if you believe in reincarnation, you still will be living a *different* life, not *this* one. Are Lila and I the only ones this has come as a shock to, or does everyone think at first there will plenty of time to start over and do it right?

What if we make mistakes that can't be fixed? What if Poppy won't forgive me? What if our friendship is over, which means this whole part of my life is over? And how will I go through the rest of my life without my best friend by my side, when it's all my fault that we aren't friends any more?

Does anyone, anywhere, have all the answers to life?

Maybe Mum knows more than I give her credit for. Maybe she's *not* trying to be smug when she's right yet again, but is just trying to stop me from making the same mistakes she made, and wishing my youth away.

Maybe.

LILA

CHAPTER SIXTEEN

MONDAY 24TH NOVEMBER 1997

I haven't written anything in here for two weeks, because there's been nothing to write. Life has continued like *Groundhog Day*, always the same – wake up, check home email for a message from Nicky, go to college, check college email for anything from him, go to classes, try to stay awake and pay attention, wonder if anything I'm learning will ever be of any use to me in my future life, hang out with everyone at break and lunch, make plans for the weekends, work on my 'personal statement' for UCAS, do homework, go to parties / the cinema / for coffee, don't kiss any other boys, try and be a good friend / girlfriend / daughter / student / generally virtuous and worthy person.

And for what? What is the *point* in even trying to be a good person, in trying to do the right thing? What is the point of *anything*?

I came home from college today, tired and weary. I

feel very tired a lot of the time right now. Mum says it's the time of year, and I should just take a multi-vitamin, but I think it's the effort of being a good person. It's very draining. And it turns out, all for nothing.

I made a cup of tea and switched on the computer before Mum got home – more out of habit than anything else. And to my joy and astonishment, there was an email from Nicky at last.

My first impression when I opened it was delight at how long it was. My marvellous letter had obviously done the trick and sparked off some actual communication!

And then I read it.

I read it three times on the computer, then I broke all Mum's rules, and printed it off on her brand-new printer that is *only* for important essays and Mum's essential printing needs – *'No frivolous printing, Lila, do you know how much that ink and paper cost?'* – because I still couldn't believe what I was reading, and I just needed to shut myself away and read it several times more before Mum got home, to try and take it in and understand what Nicky was saying.

Lila,

I can't believe I'm writing this. How could you do this to me? How could you let me think you cared on the one hand, and on the other, rub my nose in what was going on, by sending me emails describing the guy you're cheating on me with? Telling me about the damn *parties* you go to with him, where you flaunt him at everyone, while I'm here, on my own, missing you, thinking you *loved* me, when all the time you've been making a fool of me, and laughing at me behind my back!

There's so much I want to say, *need* to say. I don't even know where to start. OK. I'll start with that last letter you sent, that made me so happy. A wonderful letter from my wonderful girlfriend. With no mention of bloody 'Ben' and what a brilliant time you're having without me, and how much fun you're having and all the parties you're going to and how great 'Ben' is and all the other crap you've been going on about in your emails. I didn't know how to reply to those emails.

Right from the start of term, you started talking about this guy 'Ben' and I didn't know if that was some kind of a hint I was supposed to pick up on, that something was going on between you. And the more time went on, the more you just talked about what you were doing, what Ben said, what happened at lunchtime, and you didn't talk about *us* any more. And I had nothing to write back about what I was doing in turn, because I'm so miserable here, and lonely, and struggling to make friends, and how could I tell you all that – you, the fun, beautiful Lila MacKay? And the longer I was gone, the more fun you seemed to have, the more your letters and emails seemed like something you would send a pen pal, and the more confused

I got, but you were still in touch. You hadn't said, 'Nicky, you're chucked,' so I assumed we were still together. Well, you know what they say – never assume.

Because obviously we aren't together, are we? Because you're running around with Ben, and God knows who else, and you aren't even bothering to be discreet about it. And you know what really hurts me about all this? How cruel you've been. I never thought you were capable of being so cruel and unkind and heartless. I knew you weren't perfect – that you were impetuous and impatient and could be thoughtless and even shallow sometimes, but I never thought you could deliberately be so petty and downright hurtful.

Why didn't you just finish it? Send me an email saying, 'Soz, Weird Nicky, you're just too weird and far away and I'm with Perfect Ben now, so you're binned, laters, loser!' That's all it would have taken. Even if you'd just stopped writing and emailing, I'd have got the message. Why did you have to keep stringing me along? Why?

You know what? Even if you had just been sending those impersonal pen pal emails, and I'd found out about this, it wouldn't have been so bad. But you took the time to write that letter, that *perfect* letter, that made me so happy, that made me think I'd been reading too much into things, that made me feel like everything was OK and you still loved me. You must've written it when you'd been with him the same day. How could you have done that? *Why* would you do that? Unless it was to string me along, the better to break my heart. Or maybe you thought I'd never find out. Was that it? Entertain yourself with Ben and keep toying with me, the stupid, devoted idiot who would do anything for you? Some sort of ego boost?

I think the worst part is how I had to find out, since you didn't have the guts to tell me yourself. Maybe you're just a coward as well as a bitch. But finding out from Rachel, well, that was a real kick in the teeth. There I was, trying to write the perfect reply to your perfect letter, walking on cloud nine – I'd even persuaded Mum to let me ring you, because I was so desperate to just hear your voice – and then Rachel's letter arrived the day after yours, sorrowfully telling me that she'd seen you and Ben kissing at Kate's party. And with photographs too, just to make sure there was no mistake.

Rachel said she was so sorry to have to tell me this. Not as sorry as I was. But you know what? (This will make you laugh, I expect. A good laugh at the stupid deluded fool's expense.) I loved you SO much that I thought, wow. This hurts. But it was just a kiss. Maybe it didn't mean anything. Maybe *he* kissed *you* and Rachel got a lucky shot at a photo.

But then I thought – if he kissed you, or it didn't mean anything, why wouldn't you tell me? I wouldn't have been happy, of course, but I might've been able to understand that sometimes people make mistakes. I might have been able to forgive you, if you'd told me yourself. So then I started thinking, what else isn't she telling me? And I sent a few emails to people at college. Not your friends – I knew they wouldn't tell me anything. Other people.

And guess what? It wasn't a mistake. I heard how Dan Wilcox came round the day after the party and found you and Ben naked in your kitchen! Even allowing for exaggeration, that wasn't a one-off kiss, was it, if you were caught with him the next day too. I'm assuming your mum was away and you let him stay over, which means it was far more than a kiss. And then I heard Josh Anderson saw you in the park, draped all over some other guy. Josh had no idea who he was, but you were pretty cosy, apparently, and tight enough with him that you'd introduced him to all your friends. *Our* friends.

That's the other thing that's killing me. No one that I thought was a friend told me about this either. Jas, I get. Kate, even. But Tom? I really thought he was a mate, but even he couldn't get in touch and tell me what you were doing. Instead, he just pals up with whatever bloke you have in tow this week.

I really loved you, Lila, you know that? And I thought you loved me, even though I couldn't believe someone like you would even look at me. I thought you were perfect. Totally perfect. But all the time, you were nothing but a nasty, cheap little slut.

Please don't contact me again. I have no interest in anything you have to say, now, or ever.

He didn't even sign it off. Not so much as a 'from Nicky'.

Once I had read it a fourth time, in the privacy of my bedroom, and its meaning had truly sunk in, I suddenly felt horribly, dreadfully sick. I only just made it to the bathroom in time. Mum came home while I was still sobbing on the bathroom floor, and agreed I was definitely not well, and had better stay off college tomorrow.

Tomorrow and forever. How can I go anywhere when my heart is broken, and Nicky hates me? And how can I fix this?

EMILY

CHAPTER SEVENTEEN

No! NO! Utterly bloody Rachel! Awful Dan! And that Josh guy must've been there in the park that day Lila was pretending Tom's boyfriend was with her, to protect them from Tom's dad! YOU DON'T UNDERSTAND, NICKY, THAT'S NOT WHAT HAPPENED, IT WASN'T LIKE THAT!

All the time I've been reading this diary, I've thought it was about Lila being sad that Nicky was away, and that she had no idea what heartbreak was. But now – wow! Now I see that she really did. Nicky and Lila were far more to each other than Oli and I were, or could ever have been. Oli was nothing more than a stupid crush. Nicky and Lila really loved each other. They really *knew* each other.

How could Nicky believe Lila would purposely hurt him like that?

Lila *must* have fixed it. She *must* have. They couldn't finish like that, it wasn't possible. A true love story doesn't just end with a misunderstanding and a crappy email. They must've made up, and then just drifted apart at university. Dad was mistaken about them ending at college. He didn't know everything about Lila then, did he? And also it was, like, about a hundred years ago, and Dad is well old and his memory is probably not what it was.

Apart from anything else, if I can find out how Lila mended things with Nicky, although it is a completely different situation, maybe it will give me some ideas about how to make things up with Poppy? She still hasn't read my message, let alone replied.

At least when Nicky sent his awful email, Lila still had the most important people in her life around her. If I lose Poppy, then I have lost the person who means most to me. I am currently toying with a plan of just bombarding her with apology messages until it is easier for her to give in and forgive me and be best friends again than it is to keep ignoring me. I worry that is borderline stalkery, but it is the only plan I have. I think maybe once an hour? When we're getting on, we message *way* more than that, so I think an hourly 'miss u so much, pls be besties again' message is fine. I will start doing that tomorrow, to give her another twenty-four hours to reply, and in the meantime, after I've emptied the dishwasher and folded the laundry, which were Dad's conditions for me staying at home today, despite the potential scarlet fever, I will read on in Lila's diary and see if there are any tips on what else I could do to make Poppy see how very sorry I am.

LILA

CHAPTER EIGHTEEN

SUNDAY 30TH NOVEMBER 1997

I honestly think I have ranged through every possible negative emotion this week. I have been sad, angry, frustrated and lonely. I have felt helpless. I have felt empty. And I have felt guilty. Guilty because Nicky was right. I should have told him about Ben when I had the chance, when I could've explained about the low ebb, and how it meant nothing other than a fleeting moment of pleasure because it seemed like so long since anyone had kissed me, and I was flattered by Ben liking me.

Initially too, I wondered if perhaps I deserved this for being a bad person. That karma was punishing me for gloating about how *furious* Rachel was that Ben fancied *me* and not her. Rachel was always so sure everyone would fancy her, with her swishy hair and her perfect French and her lawyer daddy, that she had pursued Ben very publicly. And yes, I had enjoyed the fact it must have been somewhat embarrassing for her when Ben made it so clear that actually he preferred me, with my social awkwardness, dubious hair and doubtful fashion sense.

So having revelled in Rachel's downfall (it was hardly a downfall by most people's standards, but Rachel was so accustomed to getting whatever she wanted that this was probably as close to one as she would get), this was surely the universe punishing me by making Rachel the one responsible for *my* downfall, because I'm a bad person. Which is unfair, because I really do *try* to be a good person, whereas Rachel goes out of her way to be awful (see getting Nicky's address from Luke by claiming she wanted to send him a copy of the college magazine she thought he'd be interested in) and yet nothing really bad ever happens to her.

Unfair is about right. After a week of trying to get Nicky to listen to me, of sending pleading emails that he is simply ignoring (assuming he reads them at all), of attempting to explain that nothing is as he thinks it is, my overriding feeling is just how *unfair* this is. I am devastated about Nicky, but I'm also so angry with him, and how sanctimonious he is being. He's blaming me for *everything*! He's refusing to listen to Tom or Kate or Jas, who have all emailed him too, explaining about the low ebb, the hot tea / Ben's winkle interface situation in the kitchen, and about

Jon in the park! The only person he replied to was Tom, a brief, cold message to say that fine, he believed him about Jon, but it didn't change any of the rest, and to please not keep pleading my cause.

I had forgotten this side of Nicky. How touchy he can be, how *dramatic*, how much he can hold a grudge and sulk. He did this last year, when he first told me he liked me, and came on super strong about being in love and all that, and I got totally spooked and turned him down because one minute he was my weird neighbour and the next he was declaring his undying love (HA!) without any time in between for me to adjust, so he had a massive strop then too, though it all turned out OK in the end (again HA!) and he's doing the same again now. Refusing to listen to anybody. Refusing to see there might be two sides to this. Refusing to concede any responsibility here at all.

And so now, mainly, I'm angry. How dare he call me names like that? How dare he sit in judgement and say this is all my fault, when *he* was the one sending emotionless one-line emails upbraiding me for my poor understanding of Guy Fawkes Night? There was barely a single sentence he wrote to me that suggested he was communicating with anything more than a passing acquaintance, and yet he tells me I'm a bad person for my emails becoming increasingly impersonal? At least I *tried*. At least I told him what was happening at college and tried to keep him in the loop so he wouldn't feel left out. And he just complains that I wrote to him 'like a pen pal'. Well, what was he doing then?

I'm sorry he's so unhappy in Ohio, and I'm sorry he hasn't made any friends, and I'm sorry it's hard for him, but bloody hellfire – would it have killed him to say that? I would have been there for him! I would have tried to help, to make him feel less lonely! Reminded him it's not forever, he just needs to get through the next few months and then he will be back here with me, and his friends, and orange squash.

Instead, he shut down, told me nothing, left me in limbo. And still I didn't give up on him, on us. I sent that last letter to try and elicit some sort of response, or emotion from him – and what did he do? Oh, he *says* he was working on a reply. He *says* he was going to ring me. Well, why didn't he? Or email, or *something*. I think he was just sitting in Ohio, wallowing in self-pity, and then having the nerve to get on his high horse because I had a brief and momentary rush of blood to the head because someone else happened to kiss me WHEN I WAS AT A LOW EBB! How DARE he!

And yet . . . and yet . . . I miss him. I miss him so much. I miss his smile, the way he makes me laugh. I miss how he's the only other person in the world as invested in Richard III not being the bad guy. I miss all the random weird stuff we would talk about, lying on my sofa, or on his bed, or under the trees in the park, holding hands.

With Nicky, it's about so much more than the kissing, the butterflies, the flip in your tummy. It's the way, when I'm with him, I don't feel like I need to be scared. And it's the way he makes me feel it's OK just to be me, that I am enough, that I don't have to try to be better, funnier, cleverer, prettier, cooler. The only other person in the entire world that I can be like that with is Jas. Nicky and Jas make me feel like me *is* the best version of me, even when it clearly very much isn't.

At least I still have Jas. That's something. She feels absolutely wretched about Dan telling everyone about seeing Ben half naked in my kitchen, and she did offer to dump him for that, but it wasn't really his fault. He had met Liam Conway before Jas had got hold of him to swear him to eternal silence, and Liam had asked if anyone had heard from Nicky, and Dan had said he didn't know, but he was pretty sure Nicky wasn't seeing Lila any more, because he'd just seen Ben Morgan half naked in Lila's kitchen.

'Because boys are *stupid,*' Jas told me in despair. 'Are you sure you don't want me to dump him?'

I was tempted, I cannot lie. If Jas dumped Dan, then we could both swear a most dreadful oath of abstinence from men forever and promise to grow old together, as it seems Jas is the only soulmate I will ever have. But I'm trying to be a better person. If all this happened as karma because of my nasty, petty feelings about Rachel, then perhaps if I can be a totally excellent friend, a dutiful daughter who doesn't cheek Mum or leave mugs to go mouldy in my room, and I dunno, maybe rescue some kittens or read to orphans or do some sort of Good Works, then just possibly karma will give Nicky back to me. It's a long shot, but it's the only one I've got. And since Jas has only just emerged from her long Man-Hating Phase, and seems so happy with Dan, demanding she dump him just because he's a stupid boy would be not the act of a good friend who deserves her boyfriend back.

Though, I can't deny, being a good friend would be much easier if everyone else but me wasn't totally loved-up.

SATURDAY 13TH DECEMBER 1997

The last few weeks, all I've been thinking about is Christmas.

In one of his emails, Nicky had said his mum was considering coming back home for Christmas, and although nothing had been confirmed because The Doom happened, I clung to the hope that they might return for a week or two, and I'd be able to see Nicky and explain everything properly and in person. I wasn't going to *beg* him to take me back or anything. I am a feminist after all. But I just needed him to know that I wasn't what he thought I was. After everything there had been between us, I couldn't let things finish with him thinking that about me. And if that didn't work, Tom and Kate and Jas (I haven't told anyone else what happened with Nicky and me, just that it was over. To my astonishment, Rachel hasn't blabbed to everyone either- I suppose she doesn't want everyone knowing Ben snogged me, not her, and it's enough revenge that she told Nicky) might be able to talk to him and make him see that I wasn't the things he had called me, and if nothing else, maybe we could be friends of some sort again, because I missed him.

I knew it was only a vague possibility, and I'd tried not to get my hopes up. But the closer to Christmas we got, the more impossible it was *not* to hope. After all, it was Christmas. The season of magic! If ever something miraculous was to happen – broken hearts to be mended, star-crossed lovers reconciled – then surely it had to happen now? (Or on Midsummer's Eve, Tom said, when I put this to him, which was not very helpful, given that Midsummer is miles away and Christmas is in less than two weeks!)

The further into December we got, the more I hoped

that I would hear the slam of a taxi door and see Nicky and his family hauling their suitcases up their front path. Or that I'd come home from college one evening and there would be lights on in his house, and he'd be back, and I'd run up the path and he'd open the door and my cheeks would be prettily pink from the cold, and my hair adorably tousled, and I would be wrapped up in a warm yet fetching scarf, and he would say, 'Lila!' and I would say, 'Nicky!' and we would fall into each other's arms as the snow started to fall and the carol singers cheered behind us and broke into a rousing chorus of 'Ding Dong Merrily on High'. Mistletoe may have been involved somewhere along the line, though I wasn't quite sure how.

Then, this morning, I was having breakfast with Mum, and she was reading through her post, which she always complains is mostly bills and boring things, when she opened a letter that looked like a proper letter, and then remarked, 'Goodness, it seems we're to get new neighbours!'

My toast turned to dust in my mouth.

She had received a letter from Nicky's mum, saying they were thinking of making the move to Ohio permanent – his dad has been offered a long-term contract and they are enjoying life there so much, they've decided to stay.

I could only croak, 'All of them?'

Mum skimmed through the rest of the letter, and said Nicky's mum didn't say, but she assumed so. They were going to rent the house out, she informed me, until they decided what they were going to do with it. Like I cared what they did with their stupid *house*, I needed to know what Nicky was doing. I tried to sound calm and casual, like I was just taking a friendly interest in the neighbours, as I enquired if that meant they weren't coming home for Christmas.

Mum said apparently not – they were going to stay with Nicky's grandmother in Shrewsbury, because she was not in good health.

Mum folded up the letter, saying that Mrs Harris had just wanted to let us know what was happening, since we've lived next door to each other for so long.

'Fifteen years,' mused Mum, adding it was nice of Mrs Harris to write and tell us their plans. 'Especially,' I got one of her hard stares, 'given things between you and Nicholas . . .'

I scraped the rest of my toast into the bin and fled upstairs.

That was that then. Nicky wouldn't be back for Christmas. There would be no opportunity to talk to him. I'm sorry his granny isn't well, *obviously*, because Good Person, but at the same, she has stolen my one chance to speak to Nicky. So after more than fifteen years of having him next door, always around, always there when I needed him, even when I was too stupid to see how much he meant to me and tormented him by calling him Weird Nicky, there would be no festive rapprochement with a carol singer soundtrack. No more sea-green eyes to gaze into, or freckles to count. No more jokes or chats about Richard III. No more feeling like I had an anchor in the storm, and a quiet oasis to retreat to when the world was too much.

No more Nicky. It is done.

For a moment I entertained a brief vision of making a mercy dash to Shrewsbury on Christmas Eve, even though I don't know where Shrewsbury is, or how to get there. In The Vision, it was snowing and we all piled into Jon's car and he drove through the blizzard, with many amusing japes and frolics and adventures, and we finally reached Nicky's grandmother's house, and then I flung myself through the snowdrifts into Nicky's arms, and he gazed into my eyes with his sea-green ones, and was so overwhelmed by the efforts I'd gone to in order to reach him that there was no need for words and he simply kissed me and kissed me while Jas and Tom and Kate and Jon sang 'Ding Dong Merrily', etc., etc., etc.

Of course, even if I knew where Shrewsbury was and had his granny's address and persuaded everyone, including Jon, to embark on a road trip through a blizzard, there's no way Mum would let me go haring off anywhere on Christmas Eve. In fact, by Christmas Eve, we will be at my granny's in Hampshire, a stout package containing a stout girdle for Granny reposing under the tree, and very small sherries being dispensed to Mum and Aunt Lucy, while Granny asks us all if we've put on weight and demands to know why Aunt Lucy and Mum can't find a man and tuts at them for having careers before making some racist comments and refusing to let anyone watch ITV because it is common.

I feel strangely calm now. I suppose this is what is meant by closure. There is no more hope, there are no more chances, there is nothing to cling to, just acceptance. Nicky and I are over, and I will probably never see him again.

SUNDAY 28TH DECEMBER 1997

We came home from Granny's this morning to find the answering machine full of messages for me. Everyone else's romances have fallen apart as well.

Tom's heartbreak might be the worst. His father came home on Christmas Eve from a Christmas drinks party at his boss's house, and knocked on Tom's door to ask if his 'chum' Lila was still seeing that boy he'd met in the park.

When Tom, caught on the hop, said yes, yes, she was, his dad looked very serious and said, 'She's a nice girl, that Lila. Stupid name, but a nice girl.'

Then Mr Williams told Tom that my 'boyfriend', aka Jon, had been at the party with his girlfriend and her parents, and he thought I should know, as apparently Jon and this girl were quite serious and had been together for a while. Mr Williams didn't think it was fair for me to be strung along like this.

Although this was a remarkably thoughtful gesture on the part of Tom's father, suggesting he is not irredeemably awful,Tom is devastated. All through Christmas he hoped that maybe Jon was pretending to have a girlfriend, to stop *his* parents nagging him, but when Tom finally got hold of Jon yesterday, he would only say that 'it's complicated' and that while he does have feelings for Tom, he also has them for his girlfriend Nicola, who he admitted he has been seeing for two years, and that yes, it is quite serious.

Tom was bitter then. It wasn't Jon being bi that mattered, it was the way he had lied, strung Tom along, like he was just a bi-curious experiment for Jon to have a bit of fun with. And worse, Tom had started to wonder that now he had a real, serious relationship, maybe he could tell his mum and dad. Maybe they'd be more accepting if they saw that this wasn't 'a phase' and that he was with someone he actually loved and who made him happy. And now those hopes were crushed too, along with his heart.

Tom was convinced he was utterly unlovable and would be alone forever. I passed him tissues as he lay in a heap of despair on my bedroom floor, telling me how hard it had been not to fall apart in front of his parents, just to make it through Christmas before he found out what was really going on – and then he'd to hold it together until he could get away from his family and be with someone that it was safe to let it all out to. I assured him he was very far from unlovable, quite the opposite, although given I feared that I too might be unlovable, I possibly wasn't the best person to ask.

Tom started mumbling about how he had wanted to write heartrending love poems, become the next Shelley or Keats – 'How can I do that if no one will even fall in love with me? "Nothing in the world is single," Shelley wrote – except me. And you.'

I was slightly stung by this nevertheless true pronouncement.

Tom was still feeling sorry for himself and melodramatically quoting Shelley at me from the floor, '"In one spirit meet and mingle", well, no one wants to mingle their spirit with mine, so how can someone so unlovable write about love?'

I had to be firm with him before he started quoting Coleridge, so I pointed out that there are plenty of ways to love and write about love. I had a sudden brainwave and reminded him about James Joyce who wrote reams of love letters to his wife all about her farting, and yet is considered one of the greatest writers ever.

Tom lifted his head from the soggy puddle he was now reclining in and looked at me scornfully. 'I don't want to write farty love letters,' he said. 'I want to write poetry. Anyway, you admitted you have no idea what *Ulysses* is about, so I'm not sure Joyce is the best example to choose.'

I felt this was rude of Tom, as he had been just as baffled by *Ulysses* as me. I tried again to make him see that writing about love doesn't have to be all hearts and flowers, and suggested he could write a really good poem about heartbreak instead. Like *La Belle Dame Sans Merci*. I felt quite triumphant with this idea!

'That's about death, not heartbreak. God, Lila, how are you ever going to pass A-level English?'

Jas arrived at that point, filled with indignation about the General Stupidity of Men, which was why she had dumped Dan Wilcox – because he was thick. 'Among other intellectual booboos, he had thought Cologne was in France!'

I opened my mouth to say, 'Isn't it?' and then hastily

closed it again, as evidently it was not.

Jas wasn't done, though, citing another example, in which Dan had been complaining he was not looking forward to getting the ferry to Belfast to see his grandpa for New Year, because he doesn't like boats.

'So I said not to worry, if it sank, the crossing was only twelve miles, so he'd only have to swim six miles to shore, and he said what if it sank a mile out, he'd have to swim eleven miles!'

Jas looked at us expectantly, for the chorus of disbelief at how stupid Dan was, as I opened my mouth again to suggest he had made a reasonable point, and was glad I didn't have the chance to say anything before Tom scoffed, 'He didn't think about just swimming the mile back? Doh.' Ah, yes. Obviously that was a better idea. God, maybe *Dan* was my soulmate, we could be stupid together.

Then Kate thundered up the stairs and flung herself in a dramatic heap on the floor with Tom and Jas, because Matthew has decided to drop out of Exeter and go travelling for a year to 'find himself'.

'What is this "finding yourself" nonsense anyway? Is he lost? Does he need an *A–Z?* Should I have bought him a compass for Christmas?'

We all lay on the floor, eating crisps and drinking Diet Coke and commiserating. I felt quite maternal towards them all, with my recent Closure over the whole Nicky situation. I still missed him like mad, but somehow, it all being out of my hands made it easier to bear.

'So here we all are,' said Tom sadly, 'staring down the barrel of 1998 like the sad singletons we are probably destined to be *forever*.'

Kate sat up, and through a mouthful of cheese and onion Golden Wonder announced that we should make a vow.

We asked what she meant and she explained we should vow to be friends forever, aways there for each other so we don't need boyfriends or girlfriends or partners or anyone else. Like when platonic friends agree that if they're still single at forty, then they'll get married, but for all of us and without the marriage. 'So we'll be some sort of commune or something?' Kate was very excited about this plan.

Tom was doubtful and expressed concerns about lentils and basket weaving.

'Not an *actual* commune.' Kate was scornful. 'Just if we don't find anyone, it doesn't matter, because we'll have each other.'

We all agreed it was a fine idea, and we duly took the vow to be best friends forever, no matter what.

Afterwards, Tom flopped down on the floor again still depressed. 'So is that it? Are we destined never to find anyone, ever?' he wailed.

He really was just being melodramatic now, so I gave him a gentle kick and told him he should be glad to have a back-up plan to take the pressure off.

Then I decided we needed to think to the future and more cheerful topics than our dire love lives and demanded suggestions for New Year, because Mum wanted me to go to Aunt Lucy's with her, but I didn't really want to.

'If your mum's going to your aunt's,' said Jas slowly, 'and she lets you stay here . . . you could have a party . . .'

I demurred, and then agreed to think about it, but by the time everyone left, I had been talked into it, assuming I could persuade Mum to let me stay at home.

'After all, Lila,' Tom said as he went out the door. 'I need *something* to look forward to!'

Mum was surprisingly easy to talk into leaving me behind. She doesn't get much time with Aunt Lucy on her own, and the thought of an uninterrupted New Year's Eve drinking wine with her sister and not under the beady eye of her sulky teenage daughter was quite appealing.

She was worried about leaving me alone, but I assured her I'd be fine, and then casually remarked I might have a few friends over. Mum wasn't fooled for a moment and immediately accused me of planning a party.

'More a soiree!' I said airily.

I thought it would have taken more argument, but Mum readily gave in, saying she supposed I was seventeen, and issuing her list of party rules. The house is to be spotless when she returns, I pay for any breakages, and she is locking her bedroom and the spare room's doors because 'I don't want teenagers up to all sorts in there!'

Mum is the BEST! So it seems I'm having a New Year's Eve party!

FRIDAY 2ND JANUARY 1998 – IT'S ALL TOO AWFUL!!!!!

TUESDAY 3RD FEBRUARY 1998

Pesto pasta again for dinner.

SATURDAY 14TH FEBRUARY 1998

Andy's Valentine's party. Shouldn't have gone. Too depressing, except Jas got off with Luke.

WEDNESDAY 25TH FEBRUARY 1998

UCAS offer from Warwick. Where is Warwick? Why did I even apply there?

WEDNESDAY 6TH MARCH 1998

Pesto pasta again for dinner. Hate pesto pasta.

EMILY

CHAPTER NINETEEN

I had fallen asleep last night over Lila's party planning, but I woke up this morning to the blissful realisation that it was Saturday, so even Dad will be having a lie-in, and I wouldn't be woken up stupidly early by him clattering around getting ready for work. I couldn't hear him stirring, and decided to be a good, loving daughter and let him sleep on undisturbed- in the meantime, I went back to the diary, eager to see what Lila and her friends got up to at her New Year's Eve party – if someone was sick behind the sofa, if Granny MacKay was furious about the mess, if Lila met someone else and was kissed romantically at midnight. But there was nothing there. Just stubs of torn-out pages, and 'IT'S ALL TOO AWFUL!!!!!' and then those strange, empty, bleak entries. Then it just stopped, and that was it.

I needed to know what was in those missing pages. What happened at New Year 1998? What did Lila do? How could Mum have given me the diary and ripped out the most important part?

I picked up my phone (noting sadly that there was still no message from Poppy) and texted Mum –

Where are the rest of diary pages

What are you talking about?

THE DIARY

THE MISSING PAGES

LILA'S NEW YEAR PARTY

WHAT HAPPENED???????

There was no reply from Mum this time.

How dare she! She knows she must respond instantly to my texts, that is *literally* her job as my mother! I, on the other hand, may either ignore her, or reply at my own convenience. The little dancing dots appeared, to suggest she was typing. Come ON, Mother, I need to know what happened, or where the pages are, or ideally both. The dots disappeared. I waited in anticipation for another five minutes and then was forced to take drastic action. Mum had left me no choice – I was going to have to RING her. Ugh.

She picked up straight away, which clearly showed she had the phone in her hand, and so her refusal to text me back was even more heinous!

'Emily, is everything OK?' Mum said, sounding confused and sleepy. 'You never ring me, you say only old people talk on the phone, which suggests you have no understanding of what phones are meant for, or how they came into existence, because –'

'Mum! I don't need the lecture, all right? I don't want this to be like that weird time you took me into a phone box and tried to show me how it worked – that was literally the most unhygienic thing I've ever seen. And also pointless, because if I don't have my phone, then I won't have anyone's number, will I?'

'What? Emily, I've just woken up, why are you ringing me about phone boxes?'

'I'm not calling you about *phone boxes,*' I was scathing at my mother's stupidity 'Mum, I NEED to know what happened to the missing pages in the diary. Where are they? Why did you rip them out?'

'The diary? Missing pages? I don't know where any missing pages are.' Mum was clearly still not fully awake.

'You must do! Why give me the diary if you'd ripped out half the pages?'

'I must've done it a long time ago. I forgot. I'm sorry, but I don't think there was anything earth-shattering in them. Did the diary help, though? Are you feeling less sad?'

'Yes, I'm feeling much better about Oli. Thanks, Mum.' But then I was reminded that the diary had also made me feel worse about the situation with Poppy.

Suddenly, more than anything, I wanted to be at home, with Mum, lying on her bed with her on a Saturday morning and drinking tea and eating toast with jam, like we did when I was little. Dad had been great and shed some light on the strange goings-on inside teenage boys' heads, but only Mum could understand what Poppy meant to me, and how much I needed her.

'Mum,' I gulped. 'I know I said I wanted to stay at Dad's for the whole summer, but can I come home? Please? I just . . . really want to be there. With you.'

After a short phone call with Dad, who also took some time to wake up and grasp what was going on, Mum arranged for Dad to take me home on Sunday, tomorrow. Dad was sad I was going, and worried it was because I hadn't enjoyed my time with him, but he understood. I know he does his best to make his house feel like home for me, but it isn't. Home is home. And home is where

Poppy is. And Mum.

'You know you can come back whenever you want,' Dad said. 'Just pick up the phone. Or text me,' he said hastily at my appalled expression. 'Anyway, if I'm taking you home tomorrow, there's some old boxes of your mum's stuff in the attic. We can take them with us.'

Mum looked gratifyingly pleased to see me when Dad brought me back, but somewhat less pleased to see the three large boxes Dad was unloading from his boot.

'Right,' she said, once we'd had lunch together and Dad had gone. 'Let's see what's in these boxes, shall we?'

'Do I have to help?' I grumbled. 'I'm tired!'

'Oh, stop moaning,' said Mum, like I hadn't just been away for two weeks and she hadn't missed me at all.

'If I help you sort these boxes, will you tell me what happened at the New Year's Eve party that made you rip out the pages of your diary?' I bargained.

'Does it really matter, Emily?' Mum said with a sigh. 'I gave you the diary so you could see that you weren't the first person to have her heart broken. And you seem to have realised that, so what's the point in going over ancient history? Come on, now what's in this box?'

The first box contained old boardgames and books.

Mum decided they must all be kept, and that we would have a weekly Boardgames Night instead of staring at screens. I started to wonder why I had bothered coming home. Dad wouldn't force me to suffer Boardgames Night! Maybe, since Poppy clearly hated me, I should go and live with him full-time and make new friends at a new school. I suggested this to Mum as a counter argument to Boardgames Night and she told me to stop being so dramatic, I was only just home.

The second box was a mishmash of old university coursework, postcards and letters. And the third box was clothes. Tragic old nineties clothes. I had a brief rifle, holding up items in horror.

'Seriously? They are the worst jeans I have ever seen! And you wore them?'

'They looked better on,' Mum said sulkily.

'And this skirt can barely even be called a skirt! It's *indecent*! I can't believe *you*, my *mother*, went out dressed like that! I'm actually embarrassed for you!' I declared.

'Oh, enough!' Mum snapped. 'Why don't you go and try some of them on? There might be some fabulous vintage finds you'd be glad to have!'

I snorted in derision at there being anything 'fabulous' in Mum's Big Box of Crimes Against Fashion. But on the other hand, it might amuse me for an hour, and I could judge Mum's poor taste. Also, if I didn't, she might make me play one of her old boardgames with her.

I lugged the box up to my room. The jeans I tried on were cringingly awful, and the skirts were not much better, but there was a jacket that was almost presentable. With the right boots and jeans, it might be OK? Although, was it incredibly sad to wear my mum's old clothes? Lila Moss could probably pull off *her* mum's old clothes, but could Emily Osbourne pull off Lila MacKay's hand-me-downs? Possibly not.

The jacket had that same peach schnapps smell as the pages of Lila's diary, so I assumed it was a perfume. If I *was* going to ever wear it, it would need to be washed first.

I put it on, and I didn't hate how I looked in it. Then I put my hands in the pockets and found an ancient packet of Polo mints. Gross! I decided to check all the pockets before I washed the jacket, because Mum would never let me hear the end of it if I clogged up her washing machine with mouldering nineties confectionery and tissues.

Another pocket contained an old photograph, a little blurred and the colours faded in comparison to the brilliant sharpness of modern phone cameras. A very young couple stood with their arms around each other, laughing and squinting into the sun.

On the back was scrawled *'Lila and Nicky, August 97'*.

I examined the photo closely. I had never seen Nicky before, and had had to use my imagination about him through Lila's descriptions. He was *cute,* in a nerdy way. Dark red hair, and glasses, like Lila had said. I wished you could zoom in on paper photos, so I could get a better look at the famous 'sea-green eyes'. But he had a kind face, and a sweet smile, and although Lila's hair was *tragic,* the pair of them looked so very happy. It must have been taken shortly before Nicky left for Ohio.

I wondered if the jacket might yield any further treasure. To my astonishment, in the very bottom of the inside pocket, I found a small wad of paper.

THURSDAY 1ST JANUARY 1998

It was the missing pages!

I had a brief tussle with my conscience about whether I should read them. But then, I reasoned, Mum HAD given me the diary to read, and had obviously forgotten about tearing out the pages and putting them in her pocket, so I wasn't doing anything wrong. I was still just . . . reading the diary that Mum had given me.

Right?

LILA

CHAPTER TWENTY

THURSDAY 1ST JANUARY 1998

I realise now that all my carefully constructed illusions of ‘closure’ and ‘moving on’ from Nicky were just that – illusions.

I’ve got through these last weeks by treating my heart the way you treat a bruise, by cushioning and protecting it and not letting anything knock it. But under the closure cushion and the convincing lines about being ‘fine now’, and ‘over it’, I had secretly hoped that I would see Nicky. That somehow, somewhere, he would find me, or I would find him, and all the misunderstandings would be explained and we would be together again.

Letting myself dwell on that tiny hope was too painful, like poking your finger into a bruised knee, but it was there. I think on some level I believed that if I didn’t let my imagination run wild, if I *didn’t* let myself hope, if I just kept on with my attempts to be a Good Person *without* any hope of Nicky forgiving me as a reward – only then would it happen. And in the meantime, I would just keep putting one foot in front of the other, and not even be vile to Rachel when she was her most annoyingly smuggety smug at me, even when my hand was actually itching to slap her stupid smug smirking face.

So I tried. I really, really tried. I especially tried last night at my New Year's Eve party.

It all started so well. Mum had agreed I could get some beer, and Jas came round to help set everything up, along with a bottle of peach schnapps her sister had got for her. We waved Mum off to Aunt Lucy's and then removed all the breakables and sorted out our CDs so we had a suitable range of music, and then put out the drinks and went to get ready.

There was no point in moping – we were on the cusp of a new year, and a fresh start – and I decided to begin 1998 as I meant it to go on, by making an effort and looking my best. So I put on the rather low-cut Miss Selfridge top that Anita had surprisingly given me for Christmas, and the skirt Mum says will give me a chill on my kidneys and the new purple suede platform boots I had persuaded Mum to get me for Christmas, and Jas did my hair and then we put on loads of black eyeliner and mascara and I had a new lipstick called Heather Shimmer, and we were both very pleased with the end result.

It must've been effective, because even Tom said, 'Wow,' when he arrived with Kate. I was quite pleased when Ben and Andy also said, 'Wow,' though I started to worry that maybe the skirt and the top were a bit much. But Jas said it was New Year's Eve, and if you can't overdo the glamour on New Year's Eve, when can you? She had had quite a lot of peach schnapps at that point.

The party went well. It wasn't on the scale of Kate's parties, obviously, but loads of people came, which alleviated my principal fear – that no one would turn up. Andy put himself in charge of the music, so that was one less thing for me to worry about, and Ben spent most of the night talking to me and dancing with me, and it felt nice. Maybe I could just start going out with a nice, uncomplicated boy like Ben, who I could like a normal amount, and we could just go to the cinema and have ordinary dates, and he wouldn't be my soulmate so it wouldn't matter if things went wrong. So I didn't discourage Ben from dancing with me and talking to me, and yes, yes, I flirted with him. Maybe even a bit more than flirted. Why not? We were both free agents.

And then, at about 11.30 p.m., the front doorbell rang.

I nearly didn't answer it, because I was worried it might be gatecrashers who would come and trash the house and then Mum would be furious and would probably never let me have another party for as long as I lived, not even for my eighteenth. But I could only see the shape of one person through the stained glass in the top half of the door, so I opened it anyway, and to my shock and surprise, there stood Nicky.

He looked awkward and then just said, 'Hi.'

'Hi,' was all I could manage back.

I'm trying to hold on to parts of last night, so I'm going to attempt to write down what we said, word for word. Maybe if I do that, it will all make more sense to me.

'I . . . I don't know why I'm here. I . . . I just had to see you. I couldn't stand the thought of coming all the way to England from Ohio and going back without seeing you, so I borrowed my gran's car.'

'I forgot you could drive now,' I said, wondering why apparently I could say nothing of use right now.

'I didn't realise you'd be having a party, though. I can go, if you want.' Nicky started to turn back down the path.

'No,' I yelped. 'Don't go. Not yet. Come in. Do you want something to drink? Beer? Or sorry, Coke, if you're driving?'

Nicky shook his head and said he just wanted to talk to me. I suddenly realised there were not many places we could go to have a private conversation right now, because my house was full of almost everyone I knew, and Mum had insisted on taking the keys to her bedroom and the spare room with her.

For a brief moment, I considered the downstairs loo, but that would put us in awkward proximity, and also I was pretty sure Luke was in there being sick. There was nothing else for it but the garden. I dragged Nicky through the hall and the kitchen, and out the back door. In the kitchen Tom attempted to waylay us, shouting with joy that 'the Nickster' was here, but I just said, 'In a bit, Tom!' and carried on into the garden.

'So,' I said brightly, as we sat down on the bench at the edge of the lawn. 'I can't believe you're here! What did you want to talk about?'

These words are engraved on my soul, but I still feel the need to write them just as he said them.

'I don't know how to say it, but I don't want things to end like this. Oh God, you're going to think I'm so stupid, Gran made us watch *Gone With the Wind* this afternoon, Mum got her it on video for Christmas, and I just kept thinking afterwards, how Scarlett and Rhett were meant to be together, but all the misunderstandings between them got in the way, and their own stupid stubborn pride as well. And I thought, Tom had explained that the guy in the park – *that* was a misunderstanding, and what if it was all a load of misunderstandings and we, you and me, we *are* meant to be together and it's just our . . . *my* stupid pride that is stopping us from getting back together, and I couldn't bear it and I wanted to see you so much. So much. So here I am, and you look amazing, by the way, and it's probably too late, isn't it? I've blown it, you're not interested any more. But I had to try, I had to.' Nicky was gabbling by the time he had finished.

'Are . . . are you saying there is still a chance for us?' I whispered, not quite believing what I was hearing.

'If you'll have me.' Nicky tried to smile to at me and then added, 'I'm so sorry for all the awful things I said, and the names I called you. I was so hurt, but I still shouldn't have said them. So . . . is there a chance, do you think? Can we start again?'

I was speechless with joy. I could literally *feel* my eyes shining with happiness as I leaned in towards him and his lips brushed mine. Before we could properly kiss, though, Tom had wrenched open the back door and was yelling for me to come inside because Jas had polished off the peach schnapps and as Tom euphemistally put it 'wasn't feeling too good'.

Nicky laughed, and said I should go, remarking that our most tender romantic moments always seemed to be punctuated by Jas throwing up, and I fled inside to find a very sorry-for-herself Jas slumped in the downstairs loo, fortunately recently vacated by Luke. I rubbed her back briefly and got her some water and then asked if she'd be OK if Kate sat with her instead of me. 'Nicky's here!' I hissed, unable to keep the smile off my face.

Jas regarded me with bleary but delighted eyes. 'Oh my God! Yes, go, send Kate, still feel sicky, but you have to go to Nicky, ha ha ha, that rhymes! Peach schnapps is not my friend!' she declared.

Back in the sitting room, people were counting down to midnight. Jas would have to manage on her own for two minutes, because I had to kiss Nicky at midnight, it was clearly an omen. I turned to leave the sitting room – at which point I ran smack into Ben.

As I tried to scurry out the door, he wrapped his arms around me so I couldn't get away, reminding me that I'd promised to kiss him at midnight. And as everyone else chanted, 'Three. Two. One. HAPPY NEW YEAR!' Ben kissed me there in the doorway before I could wriggle free.

I pushed him away, panting that I wasn't meant to kiss him, and he just kept saying I'd promised and trying to kiss me again, so I gave him a shove and pushed past him into the hall. But I was too late. Nicky was standing in the kitchen door. His face was very still and his eyes very blank.

I tried to explain that it wasn't what it looked like, but he just said he was going, and he hadn't meant to interrupt my plans for the night.

When I wailed at him to wait, because what had just happened didn't mean anything, it wasn't what it looked like, Nicky turned from the front door and looked at me sadly.

'Frankly, I don't give a damn,' he said, and opened the door and walked out.

I tried to chase him, but Jas had lurched out of the loo and hung onto me while she grabbed the umbrella stand to be sick into. I thrust her at the nearest partygoer with instructions to look after her and hurtled after Nicky.

Seeing the red taillights of a car turning the corner at the end of the road, I ran after it as fast as I could, which was not an easy feat in platform boots, in case Nicky had just driven round the corner out of sight and stopped to lick his wounds. But by the time I got there, his car was long gone. I stood there in despair, hoping by sheer willpower I could make him turn round and come back, but he didn't.

I don't know how long I stood there before I felt someone put a coat around my shoulders. It had started to rain, but I hadn't noticed. It was Tom who had brought me the coat.

'Come on,' he said. 'You'll freeze out here.'

I obediently followed Tom back to the house, unable to believe what had just happened. Nicky had been there, and then he had gone. There had been a brief joyful moment of hope between us, and then it was all over again.

Tom told me that Ben felt awful and had had no idea Nicky was there. That was little consolation. However awful Ben might feel was nothing compared to how miserable I was. Does this keep happening to me because I am a terrible person? Is it karma?

Tom seemed to think it would be comforting to say no, I wasn't, it was just that love was a lot more complicated and messy than poems made out. It didn't help.

I feel sick every time I think of last night. I thought perhaps if I wrote it all down, I would feel better, but it has dredged up the pain all over again.

I think I'm going to tear these pages out. Now I look at it in black and white, I don't want to be reminded of what happened every time I open my diary. I will put these pages somewhere I won't look for ages, until I'm ready to deal with what happened last night. I know- they can go in the pocket of my summer jacket. In the meantime, Nicky is lost to me forever. I just have to learn to accept it and move on.

I don't think I will ever love anyone again, though, quite like I love him.

EMILY

CHAPTER TWENTY-ONE

I was crying when I finished the pages.

Poor Lila. Poor Nicky. They so nearly made it. But what did he expect – that Lila would be a nun for the rest of her life *just in case* he deigned to appear? Lila kissing Ben at midnight was somewhat suboptimal, but couldn't Nicky have stuck around and got over it? If he really loved her? At the very least, Lila deserved to explain.

What the pages did clear up though, was why Mum cried her eyes out over *Gone With the Wind* every New Year's Eve, even though I had repeatedly explained to her that it is now considered quite a problematic film. Mum would just sniffle and gulp that it was also a classic love story, and Scarlett and Rhett were the ultimate anti-heroine and hero, and also the dresses were nice. And then I would point out that nice dresses do not excuse the racism and Mum would tell me to just let her watch it once a year without judgement, *please*.

Now I realise that she watches it to remind her of the last time she saw Nicky, despite the way they parted, despite him leaving her standing alone in the rain and the cold, despite him never getting in touch again and leaving her forever wondering what might have been.

Did she still love him? Did she still wish things had worked out with him? Or was the annual *Gone With the Wind* watch just a bit of nostalgia for her lost youth?

I picked up the pages and went downstairs to ask her.

Mum looked up in delight as I walked into the kitchen. 'My old jacket!' she said. 'It looks great on you!' As I got closer, she wrinkled her nose. 'Though it could do with a wash, gosh, it still *reeks* of Ex'cla-ma'tion!'

'What?'

'The perfume we all doused ourselves with in the nineties,' she explained. 'It smelled like peach schnapps, which for some reason we thought was a good thing.'

She fussed around, putting the jacket in the washing machine, fretting about whether it would shrink, asking if I had checked the pockets. I told her that I had, and then I held out the diary pages.

Mum was suddenly very still. In fact, she looked so odd that I decided I wouldn't give her the photo just yet, in case it tipped her right over the edge.

'Do you want them?' I said carefully. 'To read?'

Mum shook her head. 'I don't need to dredge all that up again. Now, what do you want for dinner?'

She rattled around the kitchen, chatting away about all the random stuff old people talk about – who she'd met in the supermarket, how the sweet peas were doing in the garden, what we should get Granny Anita for her birthday. I was fairly sure she was just talking for the sake of talking. Finally, she put a plate of my favourite pasta in front of me, said how nice it was to have me home, and stopped to draw a breath.

I saw my opportunity and said, as soon as Mum had a mouthful of pasta, 'Mum, are you still in love with Nicky?'

This was perhaps not my best plan ever, because of course she promptly choked, and there was a lot of coughing and water gulping, and then she attempted to change the subject, but I was not to be deflected. Making sure this time that she didn't have any choking hazards to hand, I asked her the same question again.

'No,' said Mum stoutly. 'Of course not.'

'Are you sure?' I said. 'It's not just me. Dad thinks you might still be in love with him too.'

Mum spat her mouthful of water across the table in a *very* unladylike way. I would definitely have been in trouble if I'd done that. She got up and went to the fridge for a glass of wine.

'What on earth are you doing, discussing me like that with your father?' she said furiously. 'That's so unfair, Emily. It's not why I gave you the diary at all. You didn't let *him* read it, did you?'

I hastily assured her that I hadn't, and tried to explain that it was just a comment Dad had made, about how Mum had never looked at anyone else in quite the same way that she used to look at Nicky.

Mum took a large slug of her wine, as I primly reminded her that alcohol was never the answer to anything. She gave me one of her Looks, and then became sad.

'Perhaps you never entirely get over your first real love,' she sighed. 'And the way it finally ended between us . . . Because Nicky came back once, that New Year's Eve, I thought maybe he would do it again. So it took a long time to get over him, because I kept hoping so much.'

'And no one ever heard from him again?' I asked.

'There was a brief email to Tom, saying he was staying in America and going to university there,' Mum said. 'When I finally stopped missing him, and being so miserable about him, I was just angry he could cut me off like that. Had he ever really loved me at all?'

I nodded and felt extremely wise that my mother was asking me this question.

'Part of me still wondered what I'd do, if he came back

into my life,' Mum went on. 'I used to watch *Gone With the Wind* and imagine scenarios where I was cold and cutting and withering, and channelled my inner Scarlett O'Hara to break his heart to smithereens with crushing put-downs. I felt he owed me a goodbye at least, the reason why he never stayed to let me explain. But . . .'

Mum took another gulp of wine and more Disapproving Looks were exchanged.

'But then your dad and I got together, and then you were born. And then it didn't matter about any "what ifs" with Nicky then, because I couldn't imagine a scenario where you hadn't existed. You were everything, to me, and to your dad.' Mum stared at her nearly empty glass. 'And I suppose now I just watch *Gone With the Wind* out of habit. To remind me of the futility of first love.'

'And for the dresses,' I said.

'Of course, the dresses,' Mum agreed. 'But you know, Nicky and I could never have happened, because if we *had*, then I wouldn't have you. Do you understand?'

'I think so,' I said. 'Don't you wish you'd had proper closure, though? A chance to explain, or to make your withering remarks to him?'

Mum laughed and said sometimes, but it was never going to happen, so what was the point in thinking about it now? 'Enough about this anyway,' she said.

'What's new and exciting with you? How's Poppy? I assumed that would be your first port of call when you got back. Is she on holiday?'

'Oh, Mum!' Suddenly remembering my own crisis, I burst into tears and poured out the whole sorry saga of how awful I had been to Poppy, and how I thought I might have ruined our friendship for good.

Mum let me cry for a while, then mopped up my tears and advised me to just go round and see Poppy, because it was much easier to talk about these things face to face than over messages, where tones could be misconstrued and you couldn't type fast enough to say what you really wanted.

I sniffed and said what if Poppy wouldn't see me, and Mum was brisk and told me that was a risk I had to take, but if Poppy was the friend Mum thought she was, then she would appreciate me taking that risk, and Mum was sure that we'd been friends too long to fall out forever.

I went to bed feeling heartened by Mum's advice and resolved to go and see Poppy in the morning.

I set off for Poppy's house with many opening statements rehearsed in my head. I wasn't sure whether to simply throw myself in her arms and tell her I was abjectly, pathetically sorry, or to fall to my knees in front of her and beg for forgiveness. Perhaps I would go for a combination of the two?

No one being home had not been part of my plan.

I was wondering whether to sit on the doorstep and wait for someone to return, or go home and come back later, when Julia Kemp popped her head over the hedge. My heart sank. Julia was Poppy's extremely annoying next-door neighbour. She was in the year below us at school, and thought that because she lived next to Poppy, she could hang out with us, even though to be seen associating with the lower years was social death because they were practically still children!

Julia brightly informed me that Poppy and her family were in Lanzarote,and she was feeding their cat. I should have remembered that they were away, but the date had completely slipped my mind.

Julia was still prattling on. I realised she was asking me if I wanted to go to Starbucks with her.

'No,' I said with a scowl.

Julia's face fell and I felt bad because, really, she is harmless. Also, I remembered Lila's theory that if she was a Very Good Person, karma and the universe would notice and give Nicky back to her. Of course, that hadn't worked out, but I decided there was no harm in trying to earn some universal brownie points in the hope that Poppy would forgive me, and I could start by being nice to poor Julia.

'Because of Starbucks being an evil tax-dodging corporation and all that, why don't we go to that new coffee place on the high street instead?' I suggested.

Julia looked delighted and said she had had no idea about Starbucks and how clever I was. I did feel quite clever, actually. It also felt rather good to have someone look up to me, and think how grown-up I was, instead of treating me like a child.

Over matcha lattes and some rather nasty organic muffins, I had another brainwave about getting karma onside and thus tipping the balance in my favour for making up with Poppy. As part of my Good Person Project, I would do a Good Deed by finding Nicky, and getting his account of what had happened between him and Lila all those years ago, so that Mum could finally get some closure and stop embarrassing me by watching racist films!

It was perfect!

Mum is *rubbish* at internet 'stalking' (that's what she calls it when I find out about people for her, while I call it efficiently finding publicly available information), but I am excellent at it. I could find Nicky, and explain the situation, and why he really, *really* owes her this, because he might blame her, but it wasn't her fault. At worst, she was guilty of not telling him about Ben kissing her the first time. The rest was just silly misunderstandings and overreactions.

It was an excellent plan.

Julia asked if I wanted to come back to her house and hang out. I decided that it was probably a good idea not to be at home with Mum while I looked for Nicky, in case she crept up behind me or checked my search history, because I'm not supposed to delete it so she knows what I'm up to. She hardly ever does check, but knowing my luck, today will be the day.

'Can I borrow your laptop if I come back to yours?' I asked Julia, and explained my plan.

'Oh my God, that is like *literally* the most romantic thing I've ever heard!' Julia gasped.

'We're not finding him so they can hook up,' I corrected her. 'We're doing it so Mum can get closure and move on. And also give him a piece of her mind if it's needed!' I didn't mention the 'and stop with the racist film' bit, Julia didn't need to know about that.

'But what if he's awful?' Julia wanted to know. 'What if he doesn't even remember who she is?'

'He has to remember,' I insisted. 'You never forget your first love.'

'True,' said Julia wistfully. 'I will never forget Jamie Foster.'

'Jamie Foster in my French class?' I asked with interest. 'Are you seeing him?'

Julia admitted she was not, and indeed Jamie had never actually spoken to her, but nonetheless, Julia was quite sure it was true love. I explained kindly that it was not love, just a crush, and she would know real love when it happened. I was *very* much enjoying my role as a wise older woman.

'But still, if this Nicky *is* awful, what will you do then?' Julia asked.

'Well, he's probably got nothing locked down on his socials, because half the boomers don't bother, so we'll just have a little look when we find him, and if his Facebook or Instagram is all, like, I dunno, right-wing memes, we just won't do anything,' I said. 'Or I'll just show it to Mum and say, "Look what a bullet you dodged."'

'What about his TikTok?' Julia asked next.

'Ha ha ha,' I scoffed. 'He's well old, he won't be on TikTok. Anyway, if he seems nice, I'll message him and we'll take it from there!'

Julia, slightly stealing my thunder as the wise half of this partnership, pointed out that it wasn't a brilliant idea for a fourteen-year-old girl to be messaging a guy in his forties asking about his old girlfriends. I had to think for a minute – and then I came up with the solution of pretending to be Lila!

'So then he'll probably be all, "Oh my God, I'm so sorry," and I can show *that* to Mum, and I will have fixed her decades-long broken heart by giving her closure!' I finished triumphantly.

Julia still seemed doubtful, but since it was more exciting than feeding Mittens, Poppy's extremely bad-tempered Persian cat, she agreed to go along with the plan.

'Except what if *my* mum checks my search history?' she said suddenly. 'And I have to explain why I'm googling random old men? I've got a better idea. Let's go to the library and do it!'

'The *library*?' I stared at Julia in disgust. She had a lot to learn. I am almost *fifteen*. Regardless of what a misogynistic idiot he may have turned out to be, I have *had* a boyfriend. I do not hang around in *libraries*.

'Yes,' said Julia. 'I've got my library card with me. We can use their computers, and then no one has to worry! After all, we're not doing anything illegal, are we?'

I offered feeble protests about what if someone saw us, but Julia was scornful and told me to stop being so stupid. So it was that twenty minutes later, we were sitting in front of a computer in the library, next to an old lady baffled by the complexities of Google as she tried to find a website to trace her family tree. The librarian rattled off instructions and then went to the front desk to check out some books for a harassed-looking woman with two toddlers.

I don't think I've been in a library since I was the toddlers' age. Mum used to bring me there all the time, and then I decided I was too old, and refused to go. But I'm not sure what my aversion was. The library is cool in the heat of the summer, and they have a huge Young Adult section, and I saw quite a lot of books on the way to the computers that I would like to read. I grudgingly admitted that this was not a bad idea of Julia's after all, and I wondered where on earth *my* library card was.

'Excuse me,' the old lady whispered apologetically. 'I don't like to bother the librarian again, but I can only remember about half of what she said. Could you give me a hand?'

Karma, I reminded myself, as we talked her through googling and registered her for her family history site. Now we only had an hour before Julia had to feed Mittens, who was very particular about her schedule and liable to savage Julia if her dinner was late. Still, I thought, we could always come back tomorrow. I liked it here.

'OK,' said Julia. 'Who are we looking for?'

'Nicholas, or Nick, or Nicky Harris,' I said. 'He'd be mid-forties by now, probably born around 1980?'

'*Well* old,' muttered Julia. 'Imagine being born in the *eighties*! Oh my God. Well, it can't be *him*, can it? Though imagine how cool it would be if it was.'

I shoved Julia aside to get a better look at the screen.

Julia's search for Nicholas Harris had turned up pages and pages of results for Science_Guy_Nico, Poppy's favourite TikTokker with eight million followers.

The library system wouldn't let us connect to TikTok, but there was an interview with Science_Guy_Nico in a big Sunday paper about his latest book, complete with photos. I had watched loads of his videos, of course. I hadn't had a lot of choice, because Poppy sent me them all the time. But even though I pretended I thought Poppy was a total nerd for her obsession with him, secretly I enjoyed the videos too. Almost everyone I knew watched Science_Guy_Nico and his mad experiments and brilliant explanations. I had never really paid that much attention to what he looked like, though I did recall red hair and glasses.

My heart was beating really fast. 'Click on that article,' I instructed Julia as I rummaged in my bag for the photo of Nicky and Lila that I had decided not to give to Mum, in case it made her too sad. I pulled it out and held it up against the screen.

'BLOODY HELL!' screamed Julia, earning her a stern look from the old lady and the librarian. 'It *is* him!'

It *was* karma! My Good Deeds were paying off! I had found Nicky, and he wasn't awful or freaky or weird.

He was *cool*! In a nerdy sort of a way.

'But what are you going to do, Emily?' asked Julia when we had calmed down. 'You can't just message Science_Guy_Nico pretending to be his old girlfriend from school, he's got millions of followers, he'll never see your message! And even if he does, what are the chances of him responding?' She beamed. 'Still, it's pretty cool that your mum had a thing with him.'

Karma suddenly went hyperspeed.

'Look,' I whispered, and pointed to the bottom of the article. 'He's doing a book tour. He's coming here this Saturday afternoon – literally *here*, to the library! I remember Poppy mentioning it, she was dying to see him.' I wondered if this was the universe's way of telling me to *listen* to Poppy in future.

We dashed to the front desk, and after much pleading, begging and cajoling, the librarian finally said that although the event was sold out, they always kept a few tickets in reserve for press or VIPs, and since we were *so* keen, she supposed she could let us have a couple of those. I could've kissed her. She said she'd rather I didn't, it was frowned upon to have the library users kissing the librarians, also it wasn't very hygienic.

I suddenly had the fear, though, that I had used up all the karma I had accrued by finding Nicky and getting tickets to his book event so easily. What if there was no more luck left, and Poppy wouldn't be friends with me again? I resolved to spend the next few days being extremely nice to Julia, helping Mum around the house, not back-chatting or rolling my eyes and generally being virtuous.

The old lady was leaving the library at the same time as us and I offered to help her across the road. She looked surprised and said she thought she could manage. Still, the point is that I offered, so that must be credit in the karma account again. And hanging out with Julia and generally trying to be a good person would pass the hours and stop me fretting until Poppy came home.

By the end of the week, I was bored with being good and Mum was highly suspicious. On the plus side, though, it turned out that Julia was not so bad and we'd had a lot of fun together.

I dickered and dickered about what to do about Nicky's book event, and Poppy. I had stopped messaging her every hour, as Mum said I was being a bit stalky, and maybe I should just give her some space, so I had. But Poppy came home late the night before Nicky was due to come to the library, and I would be able to talk to her in person then. Poppy would be at the library too, of course, but should I try and apologise to her before or after I explained about Mum to Nicky? What would use up more luck?

I decided that if I could get Nicky onside to talk to Mum, that would count as a Good Deed, because I was doing it for her, and thus it would provide me with extra karma for apologising to Poppy, so *after* I'd sorted the Nicky situation, I would talk to Poppy and grovel like the worm I am.

In the end, though, it was out of my hands, because as I tried to scuttle past Poppy's house on the way to collect Julia, I saw Poppy looking out of her sitting-room window, and we somehow made eye contact. I couldn't just walk on to Julia's then and only talk to Poppy later at the library, it would look too weird. So I took a deep breath and walked up the front path.

Before I could ring the doorbell, Poppy flung the door open and wailed, 'Emily! You're here! How did you know?' And burst into floods of tears.

After Poppy had calmed down, she hiccupped out the sorry tale of the perfidy of Grace Walker. Grace had seemed the perfect new friend, encouraging Poppy to audition for parts in the theatre summer school show, suggesting new make-up and hair tips, and proffering wise sixteen-year-old advice to the secrets Poppy confided in her. When Poppy was given the part that Grace had wanted, Grace was sweetness and light, assuring Poppy that she was thrilled for her.

And then, this morning, Poppy had picked up her phone to find that Ellie Carmichael had accidently added Poppy to a Snapchat group called Poopy Poppy, the entire purpose of which was for Grace to slag off Poppy to her friends, and share all those confidences Poppy had told her, making fun of Poppy's appearance and clothes, and calling Poppy everything under the sun for 'stealing' the part that Grace had considered 'hers'. Worst of all, Grace had bragged about how she had told Niall Allinson, Poppy's secret crush, that Poppy liked him. Awful Alexa Neville was part of the group too, obviously.

Poppy, understandably, was devastated and humiliated and furious and mortified all at once.

'And all I could think was how you would never ever have done anything like that to me, and you had been right about Grace all along. She was VILE, and no wonder you hated me for being friends with her. I should never have fallen for all her horrible lies,' Poppy sobbed. 'And I'd been missing you ever since you first messaged to apologise, but Grace kept talking me out of making up with you, so I'd tell *her* all my secrets instead, and now she and her friends are all being nasty and laughing at me. I wish I'd never listened to her. She even persuaded me to take myself off our circle on Life360. I've missed you so much, and today, all I wanted was my best friend but I'd been ignoring all your messages and then you stopped texting at all, and I was so worried you hated me now, because you were right, I shouldn't have been friends with Grace, but even though I was, you *don't* hate me, you just knew I needed you, like telepathy and you were just here!'

'Well,' I said awkwardly. 'I was actually on my way to Julia's.'

This set Poppy off sobbing again, in case she'd been replaced by Julia, and I assured her that no one could replace her, but I had arranged to go to this thing at the library later today.

'Science_Guy_Nico?' sniffed Poppy. 'I'm supposed to be going to that too. I was so excited when I got a ticket for that, and I wished you could go too, but you'd said you'd be at your dad's all summer but but how can I go now, when everyone there will be laughing at me?'

'You will come with me and Julia, and we will style it out, and we will show everyone that we don't care what someone like Grace Walker says or does,' I said firmly. 'We are better than her and Ellie Carmichael and all her nasty, spiteful, bitchy little friends, and karma will get her, I bet. Mum says if you write someone's name on a piece of paper and put it in a drawer, they will die. Let's try that!'

Poppy looked startled. 'Isn't that a bit strong?'

'We all die in the end,' I said in the wise voice I used to

Julia, 'and she deserves it. Go and get ready, Pops, because I really need to go to this thing. I've got *so* much to tell you about Science_Guy_Nico!'

We collected Julia and filled Poppy in on our plan for Nicky. Poppy was completely stunned that her favourite TikTokker was my mother's ex. 'They're like star-crossed lovers and you're going to get them back together,' she sighed dreamily.

'No! I just need to get closure for Mum!' I insisted. Though I had noticed the article about Nicky described him as single.

'But just imagine how mad Grace would be if Science_Guy_Nico became your stepdad and *we* got to hang out with him,' Poppy sighed. 'So he would take us to all those cool TikTok events where we would meet loads of other TikTokkers and probably actual film stars and stuff too, and then Grace would be sorry for being such a bitch!'

Poppy was well away now. I had to confess her Vision was very appealing, but I didn't think I could use my mother's love life to score cool points at school. On the other hand, using it to spite Grace Walker for Poppy's sake might be different.

Of course, all this depended on whether Nicky would even talk to us, or to Mum, or if he even remembered who she was.

When we arrived, the library was already packed with almost our whole school. Or at least most of our year and the years above and below. Niall Allinson was there, and Poppy nearly fled in tears of mortification again, but I hissed at her to simply ignore him, and to concentrate on looking like we were having an amazing time and didn't have a care in the world and hadn't even noticed he was there.

Oli was there too, to my surprise, as it was all a bit intellectual for someone like him. Seeing him again, I was astonished I had wasted so much time crying over someone so ordinary-looking. He'd had a very unflattering haircut, I noted with some glee. And how had I never noticed what a weak chin he had? We saw Ellie Carmichael too, who at the least had the grace (if you'll pardon the pun) to look sheepish and refuse to catch Poppy's eye as she scuttled off to the seats furthest away from us.

Once Nicky stood up to talk, we didn't have to pretend to be having fun, though. He was so funny and interesting, we all genuinely enjoyed ourselves. No wonder Lila had been miserable without him. He was really cool.

Afterwards, we bought copies of his book and joined the queue to get them signed, as this seemed like the simplest route to actually talking to him. Julia suggested being last in the queue, so we weren't hurried along.

She can be annoyingly full of good ideas.

The queue took ages. Poppy got more and more agitated that everyone was talking about her, and it became increasingly hard for Julia and I to stop her bolting. Things came to a head when Ellie, who had been a few people in front of us in the queue, passed us on the way out. Poppy gave a low moan of despair, so I gripped her hand. Then she turned fully pea green when Ellie stopped beside us and shuffled her feet awkwardly.

'Um, Poppy?' Ellie finally said. 'I just wanted to say I'm really sorry about what happened. I've left the group now, and told Grace I didn't think she should be saying those things. I never should have joined in, and I'm really, really sorry.'

'You should be!' I snapped. 'It was horrible of Grace and it was horrible of all of you who joined in. You should all be ashamed of yourselves!'

'I am,' muttered Ellie.

Julia nudged me, because it was finally our turn to see Nicky.

'We have to go,' I said haughtily. 'Come on, Poppy, Julia!'

The adrenaline of the encounter with Ellie had left my heart hammering and my mouth dry, and I completely forgot all the things I was going to say to Nicky when we got to the table where he was signing books. He looked exhausted and barely glanced up as he held his hand out for my book.

'What would you like in it?' he said, sounding like he was on autopilot.

I panicked. Still discombobulated by Ellie and starstruck by her TikTok hero, Poppy was also speechless.

'To Lila, please,' Julia said firmly, coming to the rescue.

Nicky looked up at me, did a double take and dropped his pen. He went very white. I realised too late that it was probably a bad idea to have worn Mum's old, albeit freshly washed, jacket.

'Lila?' he croaked. 'It can't be. You can't be. Is this some sort of sick joke?' He blinked hard and took his glasses off and rubbed his eyes. 'I'm sorry. I'm very tired, and I'm seeing things. It's just . . . you look so much like someone I used to know, it spooked me.'

'Lila MacKay?' I managed to say.

Nicky went even whiter. 'How do you . . . what do you mean? Oh God, am I having a breakdown?'

Julia rushed to the rescue again, as I still didn't seem able to say much.

'This is Emily,' she said. 'Lila is her mum. We wanted to talk to you because we don't think Lila can get over you until she has closure, and so we need you to explain why you just ran off and then she will stop watching *Gone With the Wind*.' (I had told Julia about that in the end, she was very understanding and said her mum watched all sorts of unsuitable stuff, like *Friends*, despite Julia explaining why she shouldn't.)

Nicky was very confused by Julia's explanation. Eventually, after some tutting from the librarian who was trying to shoo us out (it was past six o'clock and the library should have closed), we all sat down with a cup of tea that the librarian helpfully provided once Nicky explained I was an old friend's daughter and he would be grateful for a bit of time to chat with us if the librarian didn't mind, and she said of course, Mr Harris, nothing is too much trouble for *you*, and then went very pink, like she fancied Nicky, which is gross because old people shouldn't go round fancying each other. Even when they're famous people like Nicky.

Nicky finally grasped why we were there, and he rubbed his eyes again.

'I don't think I can be much help there,' he said. 'I wish I could explain it to myself, other than I was eighteen years old, and so in love with Lila that it physically hurt. And when you're eighteen and stupidly in love with someone, well, you want them to be perfect. And no one can live up to that. So when Lila made some stupid mistakes, even if they weren't her fault – yes, I know, you've mentioned the low ebb quite a few times, Emily –'

I had opened my mouth to remind him of this, but now I closed it again.

Nicky went on – 'despite the low ebb, I was so hurt by her. And I don't know what hurt me more, the whole thing with Ben – yes, you've explained that too, about the kitchen trousers-off thing, and the equipment scalding – or that she wasn't perfect. She was supposed to be my soulmate, so how could she do that to me? That's how you think when you're eighteen and you're so in love you think you might die of it.'

I wondered what it would be like, to feel like that.

Nicky grimaced. 'By the time that acute pain had faded to, oh I don't know, a dull ache, and I realised that even your soulmate can hurt you, and I was older and wiser, and realised how much of the blame for what happened lay with me, well – it was too late. I came back to England once, when we were all at university, to see Lila and to try and tell her I still loved her and to ask if she would forgive me, but I heard she was seeing Andy by then. I ran into Luke a few years later, and he said her and Andy broke up while they were still at uni, but the time I mustered the courage to look her up on Facebook, well, she had married Andy, so I thought Luke must've been mistaken. And I thought if she's happy and settled, what right have I got to go and disrupt her life after all this time?'

'Well, you should tell her all that!' I burst out. 'Even if it is just about how messy and complicated love is and you weren't old enough to know that – you should tell her! And about how you tried to come back and find her!'

Nicky shook his head. 'I don't think your father would like that very much.'

'Oh, they're divorced,' I said cheerfully. 'Didn't I mention that?'

Nicky rubbed his eyes harder. 'No, Emily. You failed entirely to mention that very important point. When did they get divorced? Is Lila's thinking about me just a rebound thing?'

'No, no,' I assured him. 'They got divorced, like, a hundred years ago. Mum's well over Dad, but Dad thinks she never got over you. Because of the lack of closure, because you just vanished. And, like you said, some of the blame for this is on you, so I think you maybe owe her that, don't you?'

Nicky thought for a while. 'Yes, I suppose I do,' he said. 'All right, look. It's getting late now, and I've got plans with my events organiser tonight that I can't get out of. And I'm too tired to think clearly, let alone make any sort of sense to Lila. But I've got a spare day tomorrow, so why don't I come and see her early in the afternoon, if she's around?'

We agreed this was an excellent plan, and said goodnight, as even the long-suffering librarian's crush on Nicky was not enough to stop her wanting to lock up and go home by that point.

We all walked back towards Poppy and Julia's road, and Julia said goodnight and turned into her house. We stopped outside Poppy's gate, and there was an awkward silence for a moment.

'Are we really OK, Poppy?' I asked her. 'Really friends again? Do you forgive me for what I said?'

'I was going to ask you the same thing! I couldn't have got through today without you!' Poppy cried. 'Do you forgive *me*, for being friends with Grace and totally patching you all that time?'

'Of course I do. You're my best friend. And anyway,' I reminded Poppy, 'we need to work together to wreak our dreadful revenge on Grace. Though maybe if people like Ellie are starting to see her for what she is, that's a start.'

We had a big hug and then Poppy suggested I text Mum and ask if I could sleep over. I had a lot of frantic texts and missed calls from Mum, because I'd turned my phone to silent during Nicky's talk, but I'd told her I was going to a science event at the library with Julia and had said I would to be home for dinner, and it was now considerably past dinner time, so she was getting worried.

To reassure her that I was fine, I made the grand gesture of ringing her, and she was so relieved to hear from me, and also relieved that Poppy and I were friends again, that she said it was fine to sleep over, if Poppy's mum didn't mind. Poppy said her mum would be the same, because she would also be very glad we had made up.

We plotted dreadful fates for Grace and the rest of the Snapchat group as we snuggled up in Poppy's room. I googled how to put a hex on someone, which shocked Poppy somewhat, but it took me to some very dubious subreddits, and once again I feared for my search history results.

'Make wax dolls of them and stick pins in them so they get really bad spots?' I suggested, but Poppy was anxious that we might get carried away and stick the pins in the wrong places so they really did die.

'Order some farting powder and secretly add it to their lunches so they spend all day farting uncontrollably and everyone calls them the Farty Gang?' was my next suggestion.

Poppy was much more enthusiastic about this. 'I'm so glad we're friends again,' she said. 'You're the most fun person to plot terrible revenge with. Grace wasn't fun at all. All she wanted to do was mess about with make-up and talk about boys. Let's never fall out again!'

'We should make a vow, to always be friends,' I said, 'like Mum did with her friends when they were teenagers.'

'I'd like that,' Poppy said sleepily. 'But not like a blood vow, yeah? You know I'm not good with blood.'

So we vowed that we would be best friends forever and nothing would ever come between us and may any who tried be doomed to fart eternally and stenchfully, and I slept better than I had in weeks.

The next day was Sunday, and Mum is usually at home on a Sunday, catching up on laundry and housework and other old people stuff. Obviously that was good, because it meant she would be at home when Nicky came round, but bad because she would be in her skankiest old jogging bottoms with no make-up on and a jumper covered in bleach stains. This was suboptimal for her to see Nicky for the first time in a hundred years.

Poppy and Julia had insisted on being there to see the reunion between Mum and Nicky, so first of all I tried to persuade Mum that she should put on a nice dress and some make-up because my friends were coming round. Mum rejected this idea wholeheartedly, and said she wasn't bothering dressing up for a bunch of teenage girls, and while she was always happy to have my friends here, they would have to take her as they found her, and then she started getting the ironing board out.

Ironing was not the answer. Ironing was the most boring, middle-aged thing she could possibly be found doing when Nicky arrived. He would take one look at her, ironing in her scabby old clothes, with her hair a mess, and run for the hills again, thinking he had been right to flee all those years ago.

Poppy and Julia arrived at that moment, and Julia, helpful as ever, announced she was thinking of becoming a stylist and Poppy wanted to be a make-up artist and they needed to practise on people if they were going to get work experience placements when they were older, and please, Lila, you're so pretty, could we practise on you?

Mum looked dubious but eventually gave in, and we whisked her upstairs, where Poppy did her make-up (we decided maybe Grace should just get some sort of disfiguring pox instead of actually dying, because Poppy had learned a lot about make-up from her) and I did her hair, and Julia rifled through her wardrobe to find something that was not hideous and did not show an inappropriate amount of flesh for a mother.

When we had finished, we stood back to survey the results. I was forced to admit that Mum almost looked OK.

'We did well,' said Julia in satisfaction.

Poppy beamed. 'You look amazing, Lila!'

We had gone with a sort of nineties vibe, as it seemed appropriate to the plan, and put Mum in a pretty summer dress, with some really cool trainers that I didn't realise she had or I would have stolen them. I had put her hair into a casual bun, and Poppy had done a masterful job of applying the sort of make-up that made Mum look ten years younger but also like she wasn't wearing make-up at all.

Mum peered at herself in the mirror. 'Wow,' she said in awe, 'I *do* look OK! Well, it's been fun, but the ironing and hoovering won't do themselves,' and she reached for her make-up remover wipes.

'Leave it!' barked Julia, who was turning out a lot bossier than I had expected her to be.

'But –' Mum protested.

I looked at my phone. It was two o'clock. Nicky could come at any moment.

'We'll hoover!' I said desperately. 'And I'll do the ironing later, after Poppy and Julia have gone. You look so nice, Mum, it would be a shame to just take it all off and go and do housework. Why don't you enjoy being dressed up and chill out?. 'You could just have a relaxing afternoon and read your book.'

'You're up to something,' Mum said suspiciously. 'You've been super nice for a week and this is very out of character. But I must say, your plan sounds lovely, so why not?'

We plonked Mum in the sitting room with her book and a cup of tea, though she had suggested a glass of wine might be nice on her unexpected 'day off', but I didn't want her smelling of wine when Nicky arrived, even if she had reeked of peach schnapps for the whole time he knew her before. We hastily hoovered and dusted, so Mum did not nag us and decide to get back into her scruffy clothes and do it herself, and then there was nothing to do but wait.

We sat in the kitchen and bit our nails anxiously. What if Nicky didn't turn up? What if in the cold light of day he had decided it was a ridiculous idea and even now he was on a train bound for Scarborough?

'Why Scarborough?' asked Julia.

'I dunno,' I admitted. 'It's far. Isn't that where Dracula was from?'

'That's Transylvania,' said Poppy.

'What if I gave him the wrong address?' I fretted. 'Or he died in the night? Or he's been mugged and hit on the head and has amnesia and no idea who he is, or any recollection of yesterday, or –'

The doorbell rang. We froze. Mum went to answer it.

We strained our ears for the sounds of an astonished reunion. All we heard was a brief murmured conversation, and then Mum saying, 'Well, thanks very much,' and closing the door. She came back into the kitchen, waved a package at us and said, 'Amazon man. Don't all rush to answer the door at once, will you?'

Then Mum decided she wanted another cup of tea, and started messing around with the kettle and poking in cupboards to see what sort of tea she wanted, and did we want a cup of tea, and the doorbell rang again. Mum was examining a packet of Lapsang Souchong, trying to decipher the use-by date (what is it with boomers and their cavalier attitude to use-by dates?) and said, 'Emily, get that, will you?'

'Why can't you?' I squeaked.

'Because I'm making tea,' Mum replied. 'Why should I do everything when there are three strapping girls here, sitting on their bums doing nothing?'

'Fine.' I sloped off into the hall and opened the door to Nicky.

'Hello!' I said in relief. 'You came.'

Nicky looked nervous. 'Of course I did. Is . . . is Lila here?'

I rolled my eyes. 'Yes, but she's being difficult about answering the door, so you'd better come in.'

I led Nicky through to the kitchen and cried in my best Emily Is Very Helpful and Has Definitely Done a Good Thing voice, 'Mum! Look who's here to see you!'

Mum swung round. Unfortunately, instead of looking ethereal, elegant and beautiful, so Nicky kicked himself for being foolish enough to leave her, she was in the process of shoving a Hobnob in her mouth straight out of the packet. Obviously, she choked again, because she's Mum and seems incapable of eating and dealing with the slightest hiccup in life at the same time.

Once Mum could breathe again, she just stared at Nicky, who said, 'Hello, Lila.'

'What. The. Actual. F–' she began.

'MUM!' I shouted, just in time to cover up her inappropriate language. 'We have visitors!'

'Emily,' said Mum with a dangerous look in her eye. 'Can I talk to you for a moment?'

'WHAT HAVE YOU DONE?' snarled Mum when she got me alone in the sitting room.

'I've found Nicky,' I said proudly. 'So he can explain what happened and you can get closure.'

Mum sank on to the sofa. 'I can't believe you've done this,' she groaned.

I smirked. We'd been very clever. 'Are you pleased?' I said.

'No, seriously, *I can't believe you've done this*. Why did I give you that diary? How did you even find him? What's he *doing* here? What must Poppy and Julia think? That I'm some sad middle-aged loser who can't even get a boyfriend and is still pining over her teenage love, so you've dragged him here to make the old biddy feel better. OH MY GOD!' Mum dropped her head into her hands in despair.

I gently removed them so she didn't mess up her hair and make-up. 'We – I – just thought, if Nicky could just explain why he was like that, and you could explain what happened too, then you could move on,' I said. 'That's all. It's not meant to be a date, but Nicky, he's never got over you either. He was telling us yesterday –'

'What must Nicky *think*?' Mum groaned. 'All these years, and here I am, a sad singleton, stuck in the past, getting my teenage daughter to find me cheap hook-ups. Also –' Mum suddenly clicked into Mum-mode – 'how were you talking to him yesterday? You told me you were at a science event at the library, and instead you were meeting up with strange men?'

I protested that it hadn't been like that at all, and explained about Nicky being Science_Guy_Nico and a massive TikTokker who'd written a book, and Mum said that just because he was on the TikTok didn't mean that what I'd done was acceptable. Then I begged her to just go and talk to him for five minutes, because why would he even be here if he didn't want to talk to her? I really thought it would help them both, and I promised that it really, *really* wasn't a date.

'Well, if it's not a date, why did the three of you get me done up like a dog's dinner?' Mum demanded.

'So you looked presentable,' I said soothingly. 'Because you'd have been furious if you had an unexpected visitor and you were in your grotty cleaning clothes. Especially when it's someone you haven't seen in, like, fifty years!'

Mum was indignant at that, and pointed out she was a long way off fifty herself so it hadn't been anything *like* fifty years, but she finally agreed to go and talk to him, 'just to be civil'.

She stalked into the hall. I followed, then grabbed her arm at the kitchen door to hiss, 'Mum, if you talk about what he does, please, please don't call it "the TikTok".'

Nicky was sitting at the kitchen table with Julia and Poppy, who were bombarding him with questions about what other famous TikTokkers he had met. Everyone looked up when Mum and I came in. Mum attempted to smile and said, 'Hello, Nicky. Gosh, this is a surprise.'

'Isn't it just?' agreed Nicky. 'You haven't changed a bit.

It's so good to see you.'

Mum snorted a little, and said, 'But why are you here?'

'What do you think he'll say?' whispered Julia as I sat down expectantly at the table with her and Poppy. Unfortunately, that reminded Mum we were still there, and she ordered us out of the kitchen.

'In fact, out all together, all of you,' she said. 'And we still haven't finished this conversation, Emily. Be back by six. And don't even *think* about arranging to sleep over at Poppy's tonight!'

We went to the park for a while, but Poppy got embarrassed because Niall Allinson was there, so then we went to McDonald's, but he turned up there too. We ended up going back to Julia's house, because her mum and dad were out for the afternoon.

'Do you think they've kissed and made up?' Julia sighed.

I shuddered. 'Ew, no! My mother is too old for that sort of thing.'

'Of course she's not,' said Poppy. 'But it's equally possible that she's told him to get out. She didn't seem very pleased to see him.'

Then Julia's mum and dad came home, and her mum

said she'd give me a lift because it had started raining, and when I let myself into the house, closing the door silently behind me, in the hope I could sneak upstairs without Mum hearing me and giving me the lengthy lecture she'd probably been drafting for hours, everything was quiet.

Was that a good sign?

At least Mum wasn't waiting in the hall, breathing fire and brimstone and telling me I was grounded FOREVER. Maybe she'd been arrested for decking Nicky? Oh God, would I ever live down the shame if my mother assaulted Science_Guy_Nico? And Poppy thought *she* had problems!

I was taking off my shoes when I heard a low chuckle from the sitting room. It didn't sound like Mum's laugh, but nor did it sound like the sort of noise a police officer would make in the process of arresting her for punching a famous TikTokker.

I quietly opened the door to find Mum and Nicky sitting very close together on the sofa. They were both laughing, and Nicky was saying, 'That's not *all* I do, Lila. I'm actually a serious scientist too. I lecture, and I've written several adult books.'

'I know!' Mum giggled. 'But I just can't get over you being on the TikTok!'

'MUM!' I said in horror. 'I told you not to say that!'

Mum and Nicky sprang apart to sit bolt upright at

opposite ends of the sofa. They both looked rather flushed, and very guilty. There was an open bottle of wine and two glasses on the coffee table.

'Mother,' I said in my sternest tone. 'What exactly is going on here?'

Mum looked defiant. 'None of your business, young lady,' she said in an attempt to regain the maternal high ground.

I raised my eyebrows at her. But not too much, because I couldn't help noticing that Mum's eyes were shining, as were Nicky's. Suddenly they looked not like two middle-aged people who were far too old for such nonsense, but like the teenagers in the photo I had found.

I reached into my jacket pocket and pulled out the photo. 'Here,' I said. 'I'll make my own dinner, and then I'm going up to my room. Keep the noise down!'

'Yes, darling,' said Mum meekly.

'So,' I said the next morning over my Coco Pops, as Mum drifted round the kitchen humming to herself. 'It was after eleven o'clock when Nicky left last night.'

'Was it?' said Mum vaguely. 'I didn't really notice . . .'

'Well, it was,' I confirmed. 'What's going on?'

'Just, you know, two old friends, catching up . . .'

Mum giggled to herself.

'You looked *quite* friendly last night on the sofa,' I remarked. Mum started to say something, but I held up my hand. 'No, don't tell me it's complicated, or I won't understand, or I'll understand when I'm older. Just be honest with me. I think that's only fair, don't you?'

'All right.' Mum sat down at the table. 'Nicky has a book tour to finish. And we don't want to rush into anything. But yes, we'd both like it if we became more than friends. If that's OK with you?' She looked at me anxiously. 'Though it's a bit unfair if you say no, given you're the whole reason Nicky was here at all.'

I assured Mum it was more than OK with me. I was thrilled for her. 'Just, you know, no PDAs or anything gross,' I said, and then Mum's phone pinged with a text and she looked at it and got more giggly than ever and I sighed because I'm going to have to have stern words with her if she keeps acting like a love-struck schoolgirl.

It was still raining on Monday, so Julia and Poppy and I went back to the library. We were getting quite friendly with the librarian, though I suspected she would not view us so benignly if she knew that my mother was now having a thing with her beloved Science_Guy_Nico.

We were sitting at one of the computers, reading the sort of magazines Mum considers unsuitable, when Niall Allinson came in with his best friend Noah Willoughby.

'This is so awful, he turns up everywhere,' moaned Poppy, 'Oh no, oh no, he's coming over. Lila, help me!'

The first thing I did was obviously shut down the quiz we were doing about 'Does He Fancy Me?'. These magazines seem to have nothing but quizzes about that.

'Hi, Poppy.' Niall shuffled his feet, while Poppy stared at the floor, scarlet with embarrassment.

'Hi, Emily.' Noah made a strange face at me. I wasn't sure if it was meant to be a smile or if he had indigestion.

'I was wondering, Poppy,' said Niall. 'If, like, you'd like to come for a coffee or something with me? Or a smoothie. Bubble tea?' he finished, sounding slightly desperate.

'What, for real?' said Poppy in astonishment.

'Yeah,' said Niall. 'If you want to?'

'And I was wondering if you'd fancy doing the same, Emily?' mumbled Noah.

I blinked at him, almost as astonished as Poppy. Noah Willoughby is gorgeous. As in properly gorgeous. Way more gorgeous than stupid Oli Letby. And he was asking *me* out.

Poppy and I looked at each other. And then we looked at Julia beside us, shrinking away and pretending she wasn't being ignored by the two boys asking us out.

I raised my eyebrows a fraction, and Poppy gave a slight nod. We turned back to the boys.

'Thanks very much, but not today,' Poppy said.

'We're just hanging out with our friend right now, you see,' I added.

It was the boys turn to look astonished. They shambled off in confusion.

Julia gave a whimper. 'Did you two really just knock back Niall and Noah to stay with *me*?' she said in a small voice.

'Of course,' we said. 'Friends are everything. Always.'

LILA

CHAPTER TWENTY-TWO

Sunday 2nd August 1998

I'm scribbling this in the back of one of my old diaries, because I feel like I need to write this down. I'm off interrailing tomorrow with Jas and Kate, and I'm giving my diaries to Tom for safekeeping in case anything terrible happens to me in Abroad. I wonder if I'll start keeping a diary again when I go to university? Maybe I'll finally become a completely different person there.

I had the most vivid dream last night, though. I was old, like, *really* old, in my forties or something, and Nicky just walked into my kitchen and everything was right between us, and we finally managed to live happily ever after. I have had enough of looking for signs and wondering if we'll ever manage to make things up to each other, but it was nice to have such a lovely dream about me and him growing old together. Maybe it could have happened in another life. Who knows, maybe it will one day? But for now, I am going to focus on living in the moment and not spending my days wondering what if, what if, what if. Tomorrow I will be in Paris, with two of my best friends in the world, and we are young and have all the world before us.

Because friends are everything. Always.

ACKNOWLEDGEMENTS

There are so many people who made this book possible, who all deserve the hugest thanks – firstly, of course, my wonderful editor Lucy Courtenay. Thank you so much for all your wisdom and advice. And the rest of the team at Electric Monkey, you are all so amazing and thank you so much – but especially Lindsey Heaven, Liz Sellen-Bankes, Madeline Adeane, Olivia Adams for the gorgeous cover design, Susila Baybars for the copyedit and enduring my ongoing addiction to exclamation marks, and Beth Mackenzie for the proofread.

My marvellous agent Paul Baker deserves a medal, as well as thanks for his patience with me over the last ten years.

And of course, my darling husband and children, who supply tea at critical moments and, in the case of the children, crucial information about how young people communicate, including the fact that full stops are now considered 'passive aggressive'. And all my wonderful friends who have proper, serious, grown-up jobs, but nonetheless listen to me complain about how hard a writer's life is – thank you all!

GILL SIMS

Gill Sims is the author of the hugely successful parenting blog and Facebook site 'Peter and Jane'. Her first book *Why Mummy Drinks* was the bestselling hardback fiction debut of 2017, spending over six months in the top ten of the *Sunday Times* bestseller list, and was shortlisted for Debut Novel of the Year in the British Book Awards. Her globally bestselling Why Mummy . . . series has now sold over a million copies. This is her first YA book.

DON'T MISS BOOK ONE!